Water into Wine

ILLINOIS SHORT FICTION

A list of books in this series appears at the end of this volume.

Helen Norris

Water into Wine

UNIVERSITY OF ILLINOIS PRESS

Urbana and Chicago

Short Story Index
84-88

For Katie

Publication of this work was supported in part
by grants from the Illinois Arts Council, a state agency,
and the National Endowment for the Arts.

This book is printed on acid-free paper.

"The Cormorant," *Sewanee Review* 96:2 (Spring 1988)
"Mrs. Moonlight," *Sewanee Review* 94:2 (Spring 1986)
"The Light on the Water," *Southern Review* 24:2 (Spring 1988)
"The Pearl Sitter," *Southern Review* 22:1 (Winter 1986)
"Water into Wine" *Sewanee Review* 95:3 (Summer 1987)

Library of Congress Cataloging-in-Publication Data

Norris, Helen, 1916–
  Water into wine.

  (Illinois short fiction)
  Contents: The cormorant—Mrs. Moonlight—The light on the water—[etc.]
  I. Title. II. Series.
PS3527.0497W38 1988   813'.52   87-34289
ISBN 0-252-01540-1 (alk. paper)

Contents

The Cormorant

One day the cormorants appeared, a brace of them first, then seven more. He saw them perched on the little rock not far away, staring intently into the sea. They were black as Satan, with arching throats and each with a strong, distendible pouch below the beak to fill with fish. Something about them echoed the war. Their black, perhaps, or the way they swiftly devoured the living and packed them dying into their throats, hoarding them there as he hoarded the driftwood he gathered to carve and packed into his narrow hut. When they'd had enough of the catch, they stood on the posts, the remnants of an ancient pier, with wings outspread for hours it seemed, as if they had hung themselves out to dry. Their curious feet, with webs between each one of the toes, unlike the other birds he knew, were locked like death around the poles. Bizarre they were, and ominous.

It was crazy to think that a bird could do it, but he found that the war was back again. At first to his nights and then his days. One day in a box beneath his bunk he looked for and found a block of ebony he had saved. He began to carve a cormorant. He cut deep and deeper into his pain and fashioned a bird as black as hell with midnight wings spread out to dry. When he slept at night he dwelt in the shadow of those wings.

He had taken up carving wood after the war to settle his nerves. It was good for that. You didn't think. You just sank into the wood a ways and lay there waiting to cut yourself. That was the way he thought of it. You were the wood and the carver too. He cut his hand almost every day. And he cut himself down in the wood, sometimes so deep he wanted to cry, and not with the pain but the joy of it. The joy of the angle that makes the wing take off in flight. Joy like that.

Most of his money he had spent for wood—walnut and ash. He practiced at first on poplar and pine. Forgiving woods, he'd heard them called. If you cut amiss or went too deep, the wood would let you make it right. But he grew to despise its tolerance. As his skill increased he had wanted wood that would hold its own. If in some way he couldn't explain, he was the wood and the one who carved, he wanted the fight to be hard and fair. And if it was, the thing that was made of the fight was good. It was one war that somebody won. Or something won.

When his nerves improved, there were times when it wasn't a war at all. It was more like a rescue mission of sorts. Sometimes when he was down in the oak, imprisoned there in the shape of a gull, he heard himself shouting, "Let me out!," and so far down he could hardly hear. And then he cut himself out of the wood with wings outspread. He smelled the sea.

When his money for wood gave out, he moved to the Gulf, which wasn't all that far away, to be close to the gulls he liked to make and to pick up driftwood along the shore, mostly cypress, other kinds as well. He became a miser, hoarding it, packing it into the hut where he lived. His living space shrank by the hour. There was barely room for his table and bunk. But it made him happy to see it there, to breathe at night its saltiness. He did not mind the sand that dried and drifted from it or the creatures that died inside the shells that clung to it and gave off a faint, decaying smell.

When he wasn't gathering driftwood or catching fish and cooking them on the rusty grill behind the hut, he lay on the beach and watched the birds. He filled his mind with the sea and sky, then sat in the shade before his hut in a narrow brimmed hat of raveling straw, and carved the gulls and plovers and cranes. His life was rich with wood to cut till it sang for him. And birds to know. Sometimes they paraded along the shore and paused before him to strut and preen and lift their wings, inviting him to look at them. When he made them into something sweet, then each was like a woman to him, to stroke and know. Often he kissed the head of one . . . The years of the war he held at bay. There was an inlet down the coast where the water beneath was cold to touch and full of all manner of rotting stuff. It was overlaid with a layer of warm and sunlit sea. He was the inlet, he deeply knew. His dreams, they never surfaced now. He never waded in and stirred.

But then the cormorants had come . . . He possessed a book with pictures of birds. He had drawn it out of a library once and then had moved away with it. Each part of the cormorant he studied with care, as he never had with a bird before. He could feel the throat of the bird his own. Sometimes he absently stroked his arms, his mind on the wings and the sweep of them. Sometimes he sat with his arms outspread. He carved each feather in rich detail and rich with the dark inside himself.

When he was done, for hours he sat before his hut and stroked and gentled it into submission. His hands released the voice of the wood, its singing voice. Each kind of wood had a voice of its own, and this was a full, deep note sustained. He put the bird beneath his bunk. But he could not keep his mind from it. It was not the war, and not the note, but the shape of the bird he could not erase. Not only the shape, for it seemed to him a living thing. He could not go on to anything else.

At last he got it from under the bunk and took it down the beach a ways to a shop that went in for the tourist trade. He had taken them once a covey of birds, assorted kinds, and struck a deal. Fifty percent of what they sold. From time to time they had made a sale. This was summer. The heavy spenders came later on. It wasn't much but it bought an occasional steak and beer, a welcome change from his diet of fish. He told the owner—Sligh was his name—that he wanted to clear a hundred from this.

"A hundred!" said Sligh. "That means I'll have to ask two hundred. It will sit here till the winter trade."

"Let it sit," said Alex and left.

On the next occasion when he went for supplies, he found that the bird had indeed been sold. He stood in the shop and mourned for it. But he took the money and went his way. He hadn't an idea who had bought it. The names of artists and buyers of art Sligh kept in a book under lock and key, so that never the twain should secretly meet and strike a deal that left him out.

One day when he was back from the store he found the cormorants on the posts and the woman sitting upon his rock. She was golden-skinned and motionless. Her chin was resting upon her knees. The arc of her neck was a warm half-moon. Her slender arms encircled her legs. He saw she was wearing a loosely gathered orange blouse and a homespun skirt the color of straw, with a fringe below. It fell away from her down the rock. The edge of it was in the water, floating like something washed ashore. The girl herself seemed out of the sea and as much at home as the cormorants. He stood in front of his hut to watch. She did not appear to notice him, but he had the feeling she knew he was there, that she had, in fact, been waiting for him.

He went inside, put down his bags, and returned to sit with his back against the hut. He took up his chisel and the gull he was making and went to work. The girl was in his line of vision and kept him from slipping into the wood. She had never moved. The waves were running along the sand, the plovers ran across the waves. The cormorants, as if by signal, spread their midnight wings to dry. Slowly then, without uncurling her golden neck, she extended her arms to the sides like wings. His chisel slipped and he winced with pain. He laid it down and watched her now from under his hat while she dropped her arms to her sides and rose with a backward toss of her pitch-dark hair. He watched her lift the fringe of her skirt and wring the water into the sea. He could taste the brine of it on his tongue. He watched her turn and come to him, her wet skirt slapping against her legs. And when she stood erect before him, her feet bare and dusted with sand, her legs slim and slightly apart as if she rode the deck of a ship, her breasts firm and all but visible through her blouse, before he raised his eyes to her face he knew it was she who had bought the cormorant.

How he knew he did not know. It was a touch along his throat. It was a tremor along his thigh and different from knowing a woman there. He sensed no more of her than that, but that he knew beyond a doubt. He found he could not speak to her, as if her presence stopped his mouth. If she had the bird she had too much. She had found the dark he had buried in it. Recoiling a little, he looked at her face. It was golden like the rest of her, and young, soft. She belonged to his life before the war. He looked away. His throat ached.

She said, "I got it out of him." It was Sligh she meant. "So aren't you going to say, 'Sit down'?"

He did not say it to her at once. After a moment he said, "Sit down."

When she sat beside him the wet of her skirt was against his thigh. Her skin had a scent of sandalwood, very faint but he knew the wood. He saw how beautiful she was, with her short dark hair and her modeled lips. Not beautiful, but desirable. Her eyes were the green of the cormorant's eyes. And then he saw that her beauty was in her bones, as a bird's was, with the plumage only a cover for it. As her golden skin had covered hers. And still she belonged before the war. Except that she had his cormorant.

"I hope you don't mind I found you," she said.

He did not say anything to that.

"I have a favor I wanted to ask." She turned to inspect through the open door his piles of driftwood against the walls. He felt her scrutiny a violation. She skimmed his face with the faintest smile. "To carve or make a fire?" she asked. "You have a lot."

He wished to god he had never sold it. He wished to god he had it back.

"My husband died three months ago. He did wood carvings like yourself. I want to sell them, now he's gone. But I don't know how good they are. What I should ask. They may not be worth anything at all."

"Why don't you ask Sligh down the road?"

"I thought of that. But he might tell me they weren't any good to get them cheap. I don't know a thing about any of it."

He wondered why she would buy his bird if she had some more she was going to sell. He wondered if his would be sold with the rest. He wished he hadn't spent some of the money. But even so, she had paid for it twice what he had got. He said, "I wouldn't be any help. I don't know much about price myself."

"You price your birds."

"Only one. Sligh priced the rest."

"I see," she said. She spread the fringe of her skirt to dry. Her hands were quick and free of rings. He felt their movement in the sand and drew his eyes away to the sea. "I'm sure it wouldn't take you long, and I could pay . . . whatever you say your time is worth. I wouldn't ask you exactly to price them. Just tell me what you think of them."

He couldn't see the point of it. She had bought his bird. She must have seen it was better than all the rest of the stuff that was sitting around in Sligh's shop. So why did she say she didn't know anything at all? And yet he acknowledged her claim on him. And not because he had taken her money but more because, like it or not, she now possessed a part of him. And he wished again that he had it back.

She stood up. "Can you come now?"

Just like that. She was looking at him and smiling a bit. "I bought it," she said. "You know I did. So doesn't that entitle me?"

He considered this. "No," he said.

She laughed at that. Her laugh was short, a rising note, like a bird's call to another bird. "But you'll come anyway, won't you, please?" She held out her hand to help him up.

He ignored her hand. He stared at her legs and thought, Why not. "Why not?" he said and got to his feet and put his tools inside the hut. "Is it far from here?"

She looked happy. "Not the way I take." She drew a sandal from each of her pockets and slid her feet down into them. Then she turned and sped across the beach through patches of seaweed drowned in sand. The reeds burned in the hot sun. He felt their heat against his hand. She crossed the road—he was following her—and took the cliff on the other side. She was cutting off the loop in the coast. She never looked back to see that he followed. She leapt without effort among the rocks. Her full skirt whirled about her legs. Now and again she held her slim arms out to the sides, as a dancer might to give an act of balance grace, or like an echo of cormorant wings. It seemed to him that her whole race up the cliff was studied. And yet he sensed her animal joy. It excited him, as nothing had done for many months. His following became pursuit. Pursuit of what? The woman herself? Or his bird in her? The sea flashed. They had reached the top. She paused for him. "Down there," she pointed, still without turning.

He couldn't see much of anything. A portion of house, live oaks and pines, the beach of course. But when they were all the way down the cliff it was clear to him that, whatever her reason for selling the carvings, it didn't spring from a desperate need. The house itself was three full stories of slate-gray stone. The grounds were a park with granite-chip walks and flowering shrubs beneath the trees. The beach beyond had a white pavilion.

She led him in through a door at the side, through a glassed-in porch past a pool of water obscured by shrubs. He saw the glint of orange fish. And then they were in a half-moon room that fronted upon the sunlit sea. The curve of it followed the loop of the coast, so that the sea in a full half-circle surrounded them.

"Isn't it pretty?" she said to him like a little girl showing off her house to another child. And then she waved her golden hand to include the carvings on table and stand, as if she brought them into being. He was amazed at the number of them. He approached them slowly, uncertain which to examine first. She followed him without a word.

"He did all these?"

"He did every one."

There were carvings of birds in many woods, some of which he did not know. There were carvings of animals, many of children, and one, a nude, seemed to be of her. He turned his eyes away from it.

At last she said, "My husband had them all over the house. But I put them in here so you could see them."

He glanced at her in disbelief that she could have been so sure of him.

She was silent, as if she read his thought and dealt with it. "I knew you'd want to see what kind of home your cormorant had." But she knew it wasn't why he had come. It was something to say. She knew her power. "Tell me," she said, "if you think they're good."

He went from one to another in silence. They were strikingly good, and more than that. They were better than anything he could do, anything he could hope to do.

"You know they're good." His voice accused her. If she had bought his cormorant, she had a notion of what good was . . . But why, then, had she bothered to buy it when she had so much that was better at home? And why had she bothered to bring him here to tell her what she already knew . . . unless she wanted to show him up? And why would she waste her time with that? One of the things the war had done was to throw things doubtful into relief and color them gray and even black. He stalked a question on every side.

There were only two things that were clear to him—the brilliance of the pieces before him, their life in wood, and the power of all he felt in her, as if she were as perfectly made as any remarkable figure there, but something you'd want to carve in wood because it could be a way to possess her . . . His eyes were drawn to the carving of her. He allowed himself the briefest glance, but it filled his eyes and filled his throat.

"You want to sell these?" he said at once.

"Yes, I do. What should I ask?"

"Ask the moon."

She laughed at him.

He circled the room. On a walnut desk he came upon an opened book. There were photographs of carvings in color and plenty of text. He closed it carefully to see the cover, which simply stated: "*Carving in Wood* by Raphael Silt." He looked up at her quickly. "Silt was your husband?"

"You've heard of him?"

"Who hasn't?" he said. He turned the pages with reverence. He kept the longing out of his eyes.

She knew it was there. "He wrote it, not for beginners he said, but for people with fifty scars or more." Her green eyes caressed his hands. "Would you qualify?"

He nodded slowly. "I'd qualify."

"Then you'll have to come back and read it some day." She turned away. He felt that she wasn't arranging it but simply waiting for him to come. And he didn't know what she wanted of him.

He looked around the room once more. "I didn't know he had died," he said. She made no reply. "Do you live here alone?"

She walked to the window and looked at the sea. "What do I owe you?" she asked him with a rising inflection.

"Nothing," he said. His hand was stroking the neck of a swan. "I've said they're good, but you knew that. The world knows that." He turned and left her standing there.

At night he lay awake in the dark, with the sound of waves, with the pungent, salty smell of the wood. He tried to recall the carving Silt had made of her; the grace of it he had caught with a glance. The woman, the craft, they seemed to be one. Then the heat of an anger rose in him, but whether because he could never hope to equal the art or because he could never possess the wife . . . it was hard to say.

In two days' time she was back on his rock. He had gone for a walk and when he got back she was there again. Ignoring her, he went to his hut and came out with driftwood, chisel, and knife and sat with his back to the hut to carve. But his hands were useless. He could not work.

His awareness of her had grown intense. She could be out there on the rock of his, a hundred feet or so away, and give him the sense that she was close, close enough for him to touch if he so much as raised his hand, to catch, if he drew a deeper breath, the sandalwood of her golden skin, even to catch the beat of her heart, as now he heard it quicken his own.

She left the rock and approached him slowly and stood before him. "Aren't you going to say, 'Sit down'?"

He raised his head. "Tell me what you've got in mind."

She sounded happy, as she had before when she stood in the place she was standing now. "What I've got in mind is this: I want you to come and sit with my house for five days. It might be six. I have to go on a business trip, and I hate to leave the house alone with all those things of Rafe's inside. Maybe I'll sell them while I'm gone. You've made me want to keep them safe. I know that you'd take care of them."

He seemed to consider it, fingering his knife. He was girding himself to deal with her. "How do you know I would?" he said.

"I know it because I know it," she said. "I know it because I have your bird."

He was slightly drunk with the nearness of her. "Where is my bird? I didn't see it."

She narrowed her eyes and smiled a little. "Of course you didn't. It's not for sale."

That could mean any number of things. "I wondered," he said. "You paid for it. You can put it any damn place you please."

She nodded her head. "And so I did." She brushed a little sand from her arm. It stung his own. Today she was wearing a skirt that was blue and a white blouse and her breasts were there. "About my house, I can pay you whatever you ask to do it. You'd have a comfortable room and bath with a private entrance. You could work there the same as here. Rafe left some wood, and he had a lot of tools you could use. If you liked them you could have the lot. You could read his book. You'd be quite alone . . . And our beach has birds that are different from yours."

"Does it?" he said with a short laugh. "Just around the bend?"

"You'd have to see." She was smiling at him with special warmth. "Don't do it for me. Do it for him, for Raphael Silt."

"You must have connections all over the place. Friends of his. Friends of yours."

She shook her head in a kind of triumph. "No, we don't. Not in the summer. They come in the winter to lie in the sun, with bulging stomachs and stringy thighs. If it was winter I could go to their beach and ask them to roll over onto mine."

He pondered the thing. If one looked at him with a cold-blooded eye, the way he dressed, the way he lived, burrowing into his driftwood at night, he did not seem like an excellent risk. He thought she must be out of her mind. "How do you know I won't steal you blind?"

"You'll come?" she said.

"When?" he asked.

"Now. Now. I leave in the morning. I'll help you pack, but you won't need much. There are even clothes in the closet for you."

Again she had been very sure of him. It might have put him totally off. But it suddenly seemed like a destined thing that he might not mind if he just relaxed. And the way she looked, the sheen of her, the way she drained and made him thirst, the way he wanted to drink of her . . . and never would, but wanted to . . . He went inside and got his things.

This time they walked around the loop. He carried a duffel bag with clothes. They hardly spoke. He thought she seemed preoccupied. When they reached the house she led him around to a room at the side, built out from the house in a lighter stone like an afterthought. It was full of light and clean and simple, unadorned. "Rafe had artist cronies of his who liked to come and go," she said. "Make friends with the view . . . I have to pack for early tomorrow. And I won't be here for supper tonight. But go upstairs whenever you're hungry, and on the porch you'll find a table with something to eat. I have someone to bring in the food."

At the door she turned and went back to him. "I forgot to open the windows for you. And tell me your name. It's on your bird. The last but not the first, you know."

"It's Alex," he said, and did not ask for hers. In the airless room the scent of her sandalwood was plain.

"Alex . . ." She said it as if it pleased her. "Thank you, Alex." Her voice was soft. "And make yourself at home here, Alex." She came and pulled his face to hers and kissed him tenderly on the mouth.

He held her, stunned with the joy of it. But she broke away. He was powerless to make a move.

When the door had closed he lay across the bed at once. It was as if he were back in the war, helpless to rouse and save himself. He heard the raucous cry of a gull.

In the morning he woke with the room alive with sun and the voices of birds. He dressed and went out and into the house. On the porch his breakfast was laid, as his supper had been the night before. When he had eaten he wandered through the empty rooms and into the room with its arc of windows embracing the sea. He studied the carvings with rapt attention, rejoicing in his liberty to hold and stroke them unobserved, to trace the features with his finger, to caress their throats, to release the singing voice of the wood.

When he came to the figure of the woman he knew, the one who had belonged to Silt . . . he stood before the silk of her flesh, her naked flesh carved in sandalwood. He did not touch it but caught the scent, and the woman herself was intensely there. He closed his eyes, then opened them to observe what Silt had done with her. She seemed to have risen from the sea with drops of water that clung to her and coursed along her thighs and breasts. He had never imagined it could be done, a woman bare but clothed in a mantle of burnished drops that spilled from peak and slipped to valley, merging, coursing down the flesh, subtly tracing the wood's grain. He stood in awe with envy and hunger. The envy-hunger seemed to spread in rivers of water through his flesh. It was in his hand that had held the knife. It was in his mouth that she had kissed . . .

He turned away. There were other carvings, some of a boy at various ages and stages of growth. But his eyes alighted on the opened book. Silt's book. It waited for him.

The book began: "You hold the chisel in your hand, your knife perhaps, whatever you have. Think of yourself as wandering through a dense forest in search of something you have always loved. It may be a bird or a child you have just discovered, but think of it as forever loved, for the moment lost. And with this sense of loss and yearning you make the first breach in the wood. You make it because there is no other way . . ."

And so he read till his eyes were overwhelmed by the flash of sea through the bow of windows. Deep in himself the tears were pooled. For Silt had written the words for him. All that he'd groped in the dark to do, Silt, rejoicing, had done in the light. Each piece in the room was filled with light, and each of them sprang from the words of the book and into life, to lead him out of the fields of bodies, out of the swamps and the villages haunted with their dead . . .

He lived for three days with the book and the carvings that filled the room. Very slowly his wonder grew until it approached a state of trance. He wandered through other downstairs rooms, scarcely aware of what they contained. The book and the carvings were all he knew. And the woman who would return to him . . . There was plenty of wood in a chest in his room and tools in a drawer of the table there, but he made no carvings of his own. Instead, he paced the water's edge and dreamt of seeing the block of wood riding the giant wave to shore and then of carving the woman with wings, black or white he could not tell, but a better thing than Silt had done.

As she had promised, the birds were different—an ibis, an egret, a blue-gray heron. She seemed to have called them up for him. Perhaps they were drawn by the loneliness. The shore was filled with a listening, as if the edge of the world were here. The oaks beyond shrank into the dusk. From the white pavilion he watched the waves. Now and again a white foam tip would become a gull, as if the gulls were made of sea. He longed to know where his cormorant was, but something forbade that he climb the stairs in search of it.

He ate the food, which always seemed to appear of itself. He would happen upon it laid on a handsome cypress table placed so that he faced the sea. Except for the birds the place was still. At times there was a sound in the house that he could not identify. Something he might have called a step, very light and overhead. Once at night when he was awake he seemed to hear a drift of music, but he knew it could have

come from the beach. Again, he caught the fragrance of food he was
certain he had not been served. From time to time he heard a distant
plash of water that was too close to be the sea. He began to wonder if
someone dwelt on an upper floor. At last he was certain that someone
did. He was content with the mystery, but he locked his bedroom door
at night.

And he let his imagination roam. Suppose that Silt wasn't dead at all
but crazy or sick or hiding out and carving away in an upstairs room.
So what had his wife gone off to do? And why was he here if Silt was
too?

On the fourth day he was on the porch after eating lunch. He heard a
sound and turned to see a young boy standing by the door. His face was
long and rather pale. His hair, the color of sand in the sun, was freshly
brushed and long for a boy's. And in his arms was the cormorant. His
eyes were fixed upon it now.

Alex stared at him in disbelief. The cormorant was indeed familiar.
He hadn't known who or what he would find for some reason sharing
the house with him. But a boy had not occurred to him.

The boy was slender, almost frail. He had a thin but friendly smile,
and still his eyes were upon the bird. "It's Thursday now." The timbre
of the voice was that of a child, but the cadence was older than that.
"She left on Monday. She told me to wait up there till Thursday and
then come down . . . Did you hear me up there? I was really quiet."

Alex nodded. The boy waited, then walked to a wicker chair and sat.
His movements were graceful but tentative. About his neck from a
metal chain there swung a miniature ivory gull. He placed the cormorant in his lap and began at once to stroke its head. "*Did* you hear
me?"

He slightly raised his eyes to Alex, who saw there was something
quenched in them, a dullness, a weary droop of the lids as if the boy
was tired of life, and yet his face was alive with his question. It struck
Alex then that the boy was blind.

"Yes, I did."

"I live here. I'm Jeremy Silt and I'm his son." His fingers, expressive and flexible, were slipping along the cormorant's throat. "The
reason you're here is to stay with me."

"I don't think so," said Alex at once. "Your mother went off on a business trip and left me to stay with the house, that's all."

The boy's smile went out of his face. But his voice was confiding and amiable. "She's not my mother. She's my step. And it's not a business trip at all. She left with a man to marry him. She isn't coming back. Not ever to here."

Alex stared. "Of course she's coming back," he said. "I'm here for six days at the most."

The boy shook his head. "It's why you're here. Because she isn't coming back."

Alex stood up, to consider the logic and then reject it. He wasn't sure of the age of the boy, who was thin, stretched out like a child who has just begun to grow, but the way he used his words was older. And the way he stroked the cormorant . . . it was like a child with a favorite toy, and yet it was like a man who carved, whose hand could know the wood it worked, where it was right and where it was wrong.

Alex crossed the porch and turned. The boy had pressed his cheek against the cormorant's beak. "She said you made this. She bought it for me. In my room upstairs I have a collection of birds my father made for me, but not a cormorant. He didn't like them. They make such a funny kind of grunt. They sound like a pig. And their feet are ugly, really gross. He said nobody wants one around, but I always did." He lifted a wistful face to Alex. "Are you interested in knowing why I did?"

"I'm interested in knowing why you think she isn't coming back."

"Because it's Thursday, and she said they'd be on the boat by then. She's going to Brazil to live. He told her all about the house and she told me. It isn't as large as this, but nice. It has a greenhouse in the back. Full of flowers, mostly orchids."

Alex's laugh dismissed the words. "She wouldn't take off and leave a valuable property like this . . ."

"Oh, it's sold," the boy informed him. "Maybe she forgot to tell you that. They're winter people, and they won't be here to live in it until the end of this next month. I wish it wouldn't be winter people. They're rich, and all they care about is lying around and getting sun. I have to stay here till my school in Switzerland is open. It's a school they have for kids like me. They all have something wrong with them. It's new, I think." After a little he went on, "My father died. She probably told you. She said she wasn't going to tell you everything or you wouldn't come. She couldn't wait to go . . . because this man didn't want her to. But she didn't want to leave me here. Alone, you know." He added at once, "When you were over here before, I heard you talk. She told me to listen, and if I didn't like the way you sounded she wouldn't get you."

The thing began to sound like a joke. "And I passed, did I?"

"Well, I didn't hear you very well, but I liked your bird." He stroked it gravely.

Alex fought a longing to take the bird and leave with it. "How old are you?"

"I'm twelve."

Alex left the house and took a walk along the beach. The sky above was the color of slate. A wind had risen. The terns were tossed and blown about. The sea was sucking at the pier. So maybe the Silt boy had it straight. Maybe she'd set a trap for him. He told himself that there was no reason on god's earth why he shouldn't pack his duffel bag and take off down the beach at once. After his piece of the war was done, he swore to god he'd never do another thing that he would have to keep on doing till somebody gave him permission to stop. The wind was driving him along the shore. He turned into it and headed back. The boy was sitting as he had left him, holding the cormorant in his arms. "Do you play chess?" said Jeremy Silt. "I taught her how."

"No, I don't."

"I could teach you."

Alex paced up and down the porch. "I've got work to do. I have to leave." Better to go and be done with it.

"She told me to give you my father's wood and all his tools so you'd want to stay."

"I don't want his damn stuff. Any of it." Beyond the porch the sky and the sea were smoldering.

"You don't like his carvings?"

Alex dropped to a chair. The wind was whipping the canvas awnings. "Are you jealous of him?" said the boy at last. "Ingrid said a lot of people are."

"Her name is Ingrid?"

"It's not her real name my father said. But he called her that and she liked him to. I like her a lot." He was stroking the wing of the cormorant. Alex watched the tender sweep of his hand. "Would you like to see the birds my father did for me? The carvings all over the house are mine. That's what it said in my father's will."

"She didn't go off to sell them, then?"

The boy shook his head. "She went to marry a man. I told you. Anyway, she couldn't. They belong to me. She can sell the house. He left it to her. Would you like to see the birds he made just for me?"

Alex stood up. "I'm leaving now."

The boy was thoughtful. "It's going to storm. We may have to batten the hatches," he said. "Why don't you wait and go tomorrow? I'll cook some supper."

Alex stared. "You're not the one . . ."

"Oh, no. Maria cooks it all. She cooks at her house and brings it here and leaves some for you and some for me. But she won't tonight. She called while you were down at the beach. She's afraid of wind. One time a tree fell on her husband." He kissed the head of the cormorant. "I cook a lot of my own stuff, though, because I don't like the things she cooks. There's a kitchen upstairs." He turned a serious face. "I really can do it. Ingrid showed me how. I read cookbooks too. I have them in braille . . . You'd be surprised at the books I read."

The rain was driving across the gray tiled floor of the porch. Alex turned and rolled the windows shut. "I'm sorry," he said, "but I'm worried about the place I live in. I may have to hold the corners down. It's full of driftwood I don't want to get wet."

"Is it really full of it?" Jeremy asked. "Full to the scuppers?"

"I sleep in one corner. It's all that's left."

"Wow!" said the boy. "That's really neat. Are you going to carve it all into birds?"

"I hope to," he said. "So goodbye, Jeremy."

"Goodbye, sir."

He was drenched with rain when he reached his hut. He slung the duffel bag with his clothes—of course they were soaked—onto the looming heap of wood. Then he took off the ones he wore and lay down naked upon his bed. Women were something you left alone. How could he have forgotten that? Forgotten the note his wife had left when he got back from a year of hell, that said she'd found somebody else. And god, the way she'd lied to him. Sending her love, all of that. Wanted to wait till he got back, strong and ready for any blow. The dark of it, the dark of her, not only the dark of his year of war, was in the cormorant he had made. Sometimes he had wanted to go too far, make a gash that didn't belong, just to get it out of himself. But something in the wood itself or in the bird protected it.

He lay in the hut with the storm that lashed away at it. The driftwood shuddered and pricked his naked body with sand. So what? he said. He's not my kid.

He didn't seem to be anyone's kid.

When daylight came he knew that, yes, he hated the women, both of them, because they'd left. And he knew that, yes, he was jealous of Silt—for his skill and the woman Silt had possessed and for keeping both till the day he died. And now he was whipping the boy for it. The storm was gone. He rose and dressed in clothes still wet and walked to the house in the morning sun. He rang the bell till the boy came down, glad to see him, all of that, holding a carving in his arms.

"How'd you make it?"

"Fine," said Jeremy. "How did you?"

"I'll have to lie in the sun to dry."

Jeremy laughed. "It was nice to meet you. I like your bird."

"Do you, now?"

"I really do. If he was real he'd gobble me up. Cormorants eat anything in sight. Their babies are blind when they're hatched, you know. I held one once. He doesn't have any feathers at all. He just has skin, all of it black, and he can't see a thing. He couldn't see me and I couldn't see him. But I felt his heart. I let him feel mine . . ."

He was holding a carving that Alex recalled, that of a boy. He clapped its breast to his ear and smiled. "I like the one you made a lot. But you know what? Just at the tail, the feathers there. My father would use a V tool there."

Alex laughed. "Well, I don't have one, Jeremy. You know a lot for a twelve year old."

"My father told me a lot of things."

"What have you got today?" said Alex.

The boy held it up. "My father did it of me," he said. The boy in ash, half reclining, was stroking the head of a wounded bird. Maybe a bird Silt had carved for him. The carving of a carving perhaps. "He fixed my eyes. I asked him to. I wouldn't have cared if he hadn't, you know, but I knew he liked to do perfect things." He came out and sat on the steps in the sun. "Did you see the one he did of Ingrid? He told me he thought it was his best. He loved her a lot."

He ran his finger across the eyes of the boy he held. "About the way she went off," he began, "my father said that she was a woman who doesn't stay long. He said he wanted her for as long as she'd stay. She went off once and then came back. He was the kind of man needed a woman. He told me that . . . Are you?" he asked.

Alex looked at the sea. "That's something I'm thinking about," he said.

Jeremy had listened to him with interest. "I thought about her before I went to sleep last night. I can really see why he liked her so much. I liked her a lot. She was fun to talk to. She played games with me. We laughed a lot. She gave me this." He lifted the ivory gull from the chain and pressed it to his cheek and lips. "If I looked at her up really close I could see a part of her face at a time. And I could remember every part and put them together in my mind. She let me do that some of the time. She said she wished she could take me with her. But I guess she couldn't be stuck with me. I guess it would be the pits for her. Having a kid on her hands like me . . . When she gets to Brazil she's going to write me and send her address. I'll get Maria to read it to me. And then we can write to each other, she said. She can't spell words as well as I can. I know that from the games we played. But that doesn't make any difference to me. Somebody like her, you wouldn't care . . . You know what I mean? You just want to know how they are, I guess. When I get to school in Switzerland I'll have some interesting things to write. She packed my clothes before she left. She got my ticket for me, too."

"Well," said Alex, "if you're doing OK, I guess I'll just be getting back. I'll check on you from time to time."

"It's all right if you don't," said Jeremy. "I don't mind it here. It's Ingrid that worried. Women just worry more than men. I remember my mother before she died. She worried a lot. I remember that. I'm sorry I talk a lot," he said. "But you're not too good with conversation. I guess you haven't got much to say."

"I guess that's it." Alex got up and went down the beach. But Jeremy called, "I really like your cormorant. I hope you didn't mind what I said. About the tail."

Alex waved and went on walking. Jeremy slipped off the steps and into the grass and called again. "I'm sorry I talk such a lot," he said.

Alex sat in the shade of his hut with the cranes preening, inviting him, then circling, calling to him *kar-r-r-ooo* and the plovers with their whistled *queet*. He took up his knife and couldn't work. He whittled his wood into curls of ribbon. He told himself she had read him wrong. She had set a trap but it hadn't worked. She could walk out and so could he.

He swam a lot in the sea now. Early morning and late at night. The birds that frequented Silt's beach he now could find at the water's edge, as if they had followed to weave him into the shore he had left. A deep unease remained with him. He seemed to hear the voice of the boy in the calls of birds and the whisper of waves that foamed against his sand at night. He worked at hating the woman enough for walking out on the both of them. And still he could have struck her down and raised her up and kissed her face. Whatever her name, whatever she was.

On the third day he rose in panic about the boy. He left the hut without his breakfast. Jeremy was in the white pavilion. The way the boy dressed all in white it was easy to overlook him there. He was holding a carving in his arms. It appeared to be the one of Ingrid. "How's it been going?" Alex sat down.

"Fine," said Jeremy. "Really fine." But he said it as if it wasn't fine, and he didn't seem inclined to talk. At length he said, "You can hold this carving. I wouldn't mind."

"What makes you think I'd want to do that?"

"I know a lot that nobody says."

"So what is it?" said Alex at last. He caught the scent of the sandalwood.

"Well, see, I took this call for Ingrid. It was these people buying the house. And guess what they want. They want to move in two weeks from now. They said they're in Maine and the summer is cold and they want to come early and lie in the sun. I told you they would be like that. They won't care a thing about the birds. It wasn't supposed to be for a while. I took their number to call them back. I didn't tell them

Ingrid was gone. It's really tough to know what to do. If I say they can't, it might make Ingrid lose the sale. She's counting on the money, I know. She told me so."

"And if they move in two weeks from now, where will you go?"

"Well . . . I can't get into the school for six more weeks, I know that much. I guess I could go to a hotel. I probably have enough money for that, but I'm not sure. Maybe I could rent a room somewhere. I'll have to pack up my father's carvings. Where do you think I ought to put them?"

"When you took off for Switzerland, where were you going to put them then?"

"I was going to have to decide."

"Don't you have a guardian?"

"I think it's a bank. I think a bank has charge of me. But I'm not sure."

A dog was running along the beach with his nose to the sand. Alex stared at the fragile boy, so pale he might have been made of sand to last till the tide should wash him away. Beneath the eyes with the drooping lids the shadows were etched and faintly blue . . . It would be easy to hate her now. "Do you have a copy of your father's will?"

"Whoever heard of a twelve year old having a copy of somebody's will?"

"You're different," said Alex. "You just might have it."

The eloquent fingers encircled the carving. "I'm not that different. Twelve years old is a big disadvantage, more than not being able to see. Nobody trusts you. Especially they don't with information you could use."

"I trust you."

"You do?" said Jeremy. "I wish you were my guardian."

Alex stood up. "I wish you were mine . . . I'll think about your problem," he said.

He walked home and looked at the hut and measured it. He could move all of the driftwood out, stack it against the side of the hut, and so make room for Jeremy. For the carvings Jeremy brought with him he would beg, borrow, or steal some crates and stack them into a corner or two and pile some driftwood over them and no one would ever know they were there. And then he would look for a safer place. With Silt dead, the carvings were worth a fortune at least.

He sat outside the hut with his knife. The cormorants had been away. Now they were back on his rock again, staring intently into the sea. He thought of the carving Jeremy held, still held for sure. He seemed to carry one all the time, like a favorite toy he chose for the day. He thought of the woman lost to them both, whatever her name, whatever she was. If he closed his eyes and opened them to find her instead of the cormorants staring into his patch of sea with eyes as fiercely green as theirs but maybe a blindness still in her that had been in the eyes of the unfledged bird, he felt there could never be words between them. Only violent and tender acts, final acts to be made in wood. He was calling up the words of Silt. In his days at the house he had learned them by heart: ". . . think of it as forever loved, for the moment lost. And with this sense of loss and yearning . . ." He stood and walked away from the words.

And were they words that Silt had made between the time she had left his arms and the time she had returned to them? And had he begun to carve her then, rising out of the sea for him, with loss and yearning in his heart?

In the early morning he walked the loop. The sun was riding the open sea. The tide receded along the shore. The waves were gently teasing the land, tossing it shells and shining reed, taking them back and tossing again and always farther down the sand. An egret strolled at the water's rim.

He saw the white pavilion first, like a shell washed clean of its living thing. There lay in wait the loneliness. The edge of the world was an edge of sand, with spume of the sea . . . and the listening. And then beyond he saw the boy. Jeremy knelt waist-deep in the water, his hands outstretched and sweeping the surface. The white shirt was pasted wet to his slender form. Alex slowed his steps to watch, then quickened his pace and waded to him. He heard the sobs. "What is it?" he said.

Jeremy choked and shook his head. Alex lifted him, dripping, out of the surf and laid him down upon the shore. He lay like a damp sea tangle of weed. "What happened?" said Alex, leaning to him.

The boy sat up and thrust his face between his knees. He choked on words. "I lost her," he cried. He was wild with it. "I let the water take her away. I wanted it to because she left. She left me here. But I want her back. I want her back."

Alex stared. Then he understood that Jeremy spoke of the carving of Ingrid. "You let her go in the water?" he asked.

"I'm sorry. I'm sorry. Find her! Please!"

"I'll look," Alex said. But his mind despaired. He stood and began to scan the waves. "Wait here. I'll look."

"Find her, please!" The boy threw himself against the sand. "I'm sorry, I'm sorry. Find her, please!"

Alex pulled off his shoes and hat. The sun was dissolving in the sea. It was in his eyes and blinding him. He waded into the shimmering light. He carried with him the child's sick heart. Floating seaweed passed him by. Ribbons of kelp would stroke his hand. A heron called. And then, far out, he caught the glint of something that surfaced among the waves, that skimmed the ripples, was plumed with foam. He plunged into the wave that threw him back to shore, then drew him forward and out to sea. He was swept from land. This hour the undertow was strong. And deep in him was a kind of elation that it was so. The sky was suddenly rich with gulls that circled him and sliced the deep. But his eyes were fixed on an object that slipped on a fall of sea and spilled to him and whirled away. Then it was gone. He went with the tide for an endless time. Around him breakers fumed and reeled. He was brimming with them and dazed with sky. The bitter of salt was in his mouth. He twisted at last to find the shore. It was hidden from sight till a swell of water lifted him. With a shock he saw the boy to his left, in his white clothes a point of light, and farther away than he could believe. In panic he began to turn, as he had turned from the fields of dead.

And again he saw it tinsled with reed, rocking gently, winking with sun . . . He fought for it, astounded by his desire for it. He did not even know what it was. He fought for the memory of something lost, the woman herself or the burnished likeness of her flesh. Or the craft of Silt . . . Think of it as forever loved, for the moment lost.

It sailed away from him and was gone. A gull banked and caught the sun and struck the water so close to him that he felt the shudder of the sea. He watched it rise and fly to land. The wings were crested gold with light. He was overwhelmed with his weariness. With only the wisdom his body possessed, without a thought he followed the gull. For long he battled the seaward drift. The war he thought he had left behind had taken him back, was his forever . . .

Like a wave he broke against the shore and spread like foam across the land. He clung to it with a wild relief. And for a moment he seemed to sleep. He seemed to dream the labor and fear. Then he raised his head and saw how far the current had driven him from the boy.

When he rose, the heaviness in his limbs was the undertow that sucked at him. Stumbling, he reached the boy at last. He sank to him and into the whisper of the surf. The edge of the world was an edge of sand, with spume of the sea. They mourned as one, their faces pressed into the sand . . .

She was driftwood now. If he waited long she might be washed upon his shore, and he would gather her, swollen, discolored beyond all telling that it was she. Until by the scent of the wood he would know her once more risen out of the sea. Driftwood was only a memory of something once alive and green. And out of the memory you fashioned another, a bird or a woman, whatever was sweet. A bird from a woman, whatever was sweet.

Mrs. Moonlight

During the night she would forget about the treehouse. In the morning when she heard the hammering, like a woodpecker gone just a little wild, she would go outside and look at Mr. Snider halfway up the tree and say to him, "What are you building?" And he would stop and tell her gravely, "Ma'am, I'm making you this treehouse like you ast me to do." And then she would remember. To forget and then remember made a wonderful surprise at the start of each day. Sometimes she remembered without having to be told. But whichever way it was, she was happy about the treehouse.

She didn't tell him that she planned to live in it. She knew better than that. She told him that she wanted it for her granddaughter Mitzi. He didn't guess she would live there to be out of her daughter's hair once and for all so the question of the nursing home would disappear.

Her daughter was to be away from home for two weeks; she sold cosmetics on the road. And Mrs. Gideon figured she could get the treehouse ready in that length of time and be all moved in when her daughter got back. So she asked Mr. Snider what his charge would be. He added up numbers in his little gray notebook with the stub of a pencil he kept hanging from it on a piece of string. He told her he could do it for four hundred if she wanted the best. If she wanted less than that, he could make it three fifty. "I want the best," she said.

"What about plumbing?" she inquired.

"Plumbing? Oh, ma'am, they got restrictions."

"It's all right," she said. "I can come down for that."

"You planning on being up here some yourself?"

"I might," she said. "You can't tell."

He looked at her slantwise. "I wouldn't recommend it."

"What about a stove?"

"A stove?"

"For cooking."

"That ain't exactly possible. Unless . . ." He consulted the sky, the tree, and the ground. He turned and spat with care on the far side of her. "Unless a 'lectrician could run a line up the trunk. You might could have a little hot plate, something of that nature. I said might. They got restrictions."

"That's what I'll do," she said.

"I said he might could do it, ma'am."

"It's all right either way. I can fix sandwiches. And I'm very fond of junk food."

Sometimes the way he looked at her she thought he might have guessed her plans, but she didn't care. He was being paid and that was that. She was sick to death of everybody dabbling in her business. Mattie the maid was always snooping. She had been told to do it. "Miss Fanny, you ain't et a bite a lunch." "Miss Fanny, I wouldn't walk that far if I was you." Her daughter was gone all day and Mitzi was in school till three o'clock. So Mattie trailed her. "Mattie, don't you have some cleaning you can do?"

Mrs. Gideon had a special treehouse in mind. She drew the plan for Mr. Snider on a paper napkin. "It has to look this way. I had a treehouse once and it was just like this. I want a window here, and just a little platform where I can sit and watch the moon."

He looked slantwise again. "I wouldn't recommend a person being up here after dark. A ladder ain't that safe."

"Make it safe," she said.

When the house was well along, she looked up one morning and was amazed to see that it was like the treehouse she had had when she was young. "Mr. Snider, this is wonderful! This is just the way my treehouse looked when I was young, the little porch and all."

"Ma'am, I'm building it the way you ast me to do."

"Did I?" she said in wonder. "Well, I'm glad." She had forgotten all about it.

But the treehouse of the past was very clear in her mind. It had been built when she was ten, and there the best years of her life had been spent. Sometimes she had slipped up to watch the sunrise. She had watched the moonrise too, heard the wind in the leaves and the tree-frogs after rain and the chatter of the squirrels and birds going to sleep, all as if she had belonged to the world of the tree. Especially she remembered how clear her mind had been. Everything that happened seemed to fall into a crystal pool and she could look down and see it lying on the bottom whenever she chose. Not like it was today. Not like that at all.

Again she asked Mr. Snider what his charge would be. Then she wrote him out a check and pinned it to the leaf of the tree he was in. "I might forget it later on. Things slip my mind." She thought of telling him that she was seventy-eight. Or was she older than that? Or maybe she was younger. She would have to look it up, but it didn't matter.

She waited till one day when the house was almost finished. All it needed was the ladder and a second coat of fern green paint. Then she made a phone call. Just dialing made her happy.

He answered her at once, as if he had been waiting. He sounded just the same, but older of course.

"Robert, this is Fanny Gideon."

"Fanny Gideon!" he said, as if they shared something precious, which of course they did.

"I know it's a long way, but I got something to show you."

"Have you, now?"

"I know it's a long way."

"Not for me. Ten miles is not far. I got wheels." And he laughed. "That's what my grandson says."

"They let you drive?" she said. "That's wonderful, Robert. They took my wheels away."

"They wouldn't try it with me. I can outdrive 'em all."

"Can you come right away?"

"You bet I can." He sounded happy about it.

She made a little note for herself and put it on the door, just in case she forgot, which she didn't think she would. It said: "Robert is coming over to see the treehouse."

But she didn't need the note. She was waiting in the swing on the porch. And when he drove up and got out of his car, she knew again that they had made the big mistake of their lives when they hadn't gotten married when they were fifteen, hadn't run away again when they were caught and brought back, hadn't told the family just to go to hell.

She had seen him the last time, oh, she couldn't remember when. She would have to ask him. He came toward her, not as tall as then, not as steady on his feet, but just as straight. All his hair. All his teeth, as far as she could tell. A beautiful man.

She stood up to greet him. "I see you got both eyes and both hands and both feet."

He looked down at his feet and then he held up his hands. "So I have," he said, surprised. And with his hands he took hers.

"But we have to wear glasses," she said, gay and happy.

"No, we don't. But they tell us to do it, and we humor 'em."

She led him out to the treehouse. Mr. Snider was standing on his painting ladder. The ladder for the house he was going to build last. Only his paint-speckled shoes could be seen.

"What do you think?" she said.

His eyes misted over. He circled the tree. Leaves were winking in the sunlight.

"What do you think?"

"It's perfect," he said, moved. "It's just the way it was."

"I thought you would like it."

"Like it! It's the best thing been built in the last sixty years. Maybe sixty-five. How old are we, Fanny?"

"I can't remember. But I know how old we were. We were fifteen then. It was the best year of my life."

He gazed up at the treehouse, narrowing his eyes. He took off his glasses and sighted through one lens. "Mine too. The best."

"You see the little porch where we used to watch the moon?"

"I do," he said.

"You used to call me Mrs. Moonlight. You said it was because my hair was like moonlight."

"It still is," he said.

"Of course it's not. It never was . . . I wanted you to see what I was up to here."

"Why you doin' it, Fanny?"

"Well, because I have a little trouble remembering things. But I remember that, up there, things were clear as ice. I could look down on things and see the way they were. And I was closer to the sun and it warmed up my brain and made it work fine, and the moon cooled it off so it didn't overheat."

He laughed out loud. "You gonna climb up and heat up and cool off and recall things?"

She laughed along with him. "I aim to do just that."

"I might come and join you."

"Do you think your wife would mind?"

"She died," he said.

"Did I know that?" she said.

"You came to the funeral."

She was silent for a bit. "You see what I mean?" It must have been at the funeral that she had seen him last. She added, "I'm sorry . . . I'm sorry again."

He put his arm around her. "It was five years ago."

"Did you grieve a lot?"

He thought about it for a while. "She didn't like me very much."

She touched his hand lightly. "How could she not?"

Her daughter came back before the ladder was made. She stood and looked up at the treehouse in the early sun. She was smartly dressed. Her face was made up with some of the cosmetics she'd been selling on the road. A purplish shade of lipstick that was catching on. Eye shadow to match. Nail polish to match. She wore white sandals, a white pleated skirt, a silk and linen sweater in a fuchsia shade, and a little white scarf to hide the lines in her throat. She left to talk with Mattie. She came out again and lay in wait for Mr. Snider. She told him she was sorry but it had to come down. He shook his head from side to side.

"Don't worry, you'll be paid."

"I done been paid," he said. "It's a shame to knock it down. I done my best work."

"Mr. Snider, I'm surprised at you. You should have known better."

"Better 'n what?" he said, indignant. "I work for hire."

Mrs. Gideon kept to her room. Through her door she heard the murmur of Mattie telling on her. When her daughter knocked, she stiffened every muscle in her body. "Come in," she said, although she didn't want to say it. She hardly knew her daughter with the purple lipstick on and her purple lids.

"Mama, I hope you know we can't leave it there."

"Why? Why?" said Mrs. Gideon. "I had it built to live in."

"To live in!" said her daughter. "When you have a nice room in a comfortable house?" She tore off her scarf as if she couldn't breathe.

"But I get in your way. You talk of putting me somewhere." She would not say the word. "I should think you'd be happy to have me out of the house."

Her daughter dropped to Mrs. Gideon's bed and thrust her face into her purple-tipped fingers. "Mama, I want to keep you here, but you make it very hard when you do things like this. I have to work. I have to travel. I have to leave you alone. And Mattie can't keep up with you every minute of the day. How could you imagine you could live in a treehouse?"

"Well, I didn't," said Mrs. Gideon, seeing how the wind was blowing. "I thought it would be nice for Mitzi to play in."

"Mitzi is seventeen. She doesn't want a treehouse. She wants clothes and a car."

"I had a treehouse when I was fifteen, but maybe times have changed."

"It has to come down."

Mrs. Gideon was holding back the tears. "Why does it? Why does it? It looks lovely in the tree."

"Because, Mama, if I leave it you'll be climbing up some day."

"How could I when it doesn't have a ladder made?"

"You will find one somehow and you will fall and I will be to blame."

"No one would blame you if I fell."

"I would blame myself."

Mrs. Gideon thought tearfully that many of the wretched things that happen in the world grow out of people's saying that they don't want the blame for something that in the first place is totally not their business. She said with dignity, "I've never even seen what it is like inside, but if you like I'll promise you I won't go up."

"Mama, you'll forget. You always forget. You light the stove and forget. You plug in the iron and then you forget. You almost burn the house down once a week. You took the bus to town and forgot to come home."

"I didn't forget. I wasn't ready."

"Mama, you forgot. You've even forgotten now that you forgot."

"I can't win," said Mrs. Gideon. She blew her nose and looked through the window. "About the treehouse, I paid for it," she said at last, "entirely with my money. I remember that quite clearly. I wrote a check."

"Your money. Well, Mama, it's your money and it isn't. Because when you spend it up it's mine that keeps you going."

"I have enough to last me."

"Not at this rate you don't."

Afterward Mrs. Gideon lay on the bed and thought that she was tired of being treated as if she were too young to have sense and at the same time too old to have sense. She wouldn't let herself believe that they would tear the treehouse down . . .

But late in the morning she heard the sound of hammering and splintering wood. And she cried into her pillow as if her heart would break.

She would not come out for lunch, so Mattie left a tray on the floor outside her room. When her daughter had gone to work in the afternoon she ventured from the room, stepping over the tray of food, and looked out the back door. In the tree there was nothing. It was as if the treehouse had never been. It was just the way the other one had gone when she was young. Gone in an hour. Nothing left.

She turned away, tears blinding her eyes. Mattie was working in the bedroom upstairs. She passed the telephone and thought of calling Robert, for he would grieve too. But what could he do? The phone book was opened to the yellow pages, and there she saw marked the name of a nursing home, the number outlined.

She was cold all over. Her fingers were numb, but she found Robert's number. "I need you," she said.

He heard the cry in her voice. "I'm coming," he said.

When he came she was sitting in the swing on the porch. "Go look at the treehouse." She did not want to see its ruination again.

He returned in a moment. "What happened?" he asked.

"She had it torn down. That's what happened."

He saw her eyes red from weeping. After a while he said, "But we can remember it. She can't tear that down."

She swung for a little, while he stood below her in the grass. "I didn't tell you, Robert, but I was planning to live there. Be out of her way. Get all moved in by the time she got back . . . It's not crazy," she said. "I was going to have a little hot plate put in. Be out of her way . . ." The chain creaked as she swung. "But now you know what? I made the thing happen I didn't want to happen. The reason I did it was to keep it away. She called a nursing home. I saw the number by the phone. I'm so afraid, Robert. I'm so afraid."

He climbed the steps then and sat down beside her. They swung together. He held her hand.

"I'm so tired of being treated like I don't have sense enough to live here."

"I know," he said. "I get it too. But when he gets too out of line I tell my son off."

"You do? I wish I could."

"You gotta have guts, the older you get." He thought of it, swinging. "It takes more guts than it does when you're young."

"If we had got married when we tried to then . . . If we had been faster so they couldn't have caught us . . ."

He squeezed her hand.

"I don't ever think about my husband," she said. "Isn't that strange? I never think about him. It was like when he died I had got that over with. I must have been sad, though. I can't recall."

They swung in silence.

"I wish I could start my life over again. I'd fix it so I wouldn't have to be afraid."

"I'm thinking," he said. "I'm thinking now. You wanta live in a treehouse? My kid brother has a little house in the woods. You remember Alfie. It's in the next county. Trees around it. You can't hardly see it for all the trees. Nothing fancy inside. He goes there to hunt in the wintertime."

She was suddenly so happy she began to cry. "You mean we could go?"

"Why not?" he said. "I slipped around and saw where he hides the key."

Her eyes were shining as she thought of it.

"You go in and leave a note for your daughter. Say you're with me and we've gone to the woods. I'll be in the car."

"I'll do it," she said. She went inside but didn't write the note. She grabbed her purse from the dresser and a sweater from the bed and slipped out when Mattie was running water in the sink. She climbed in beside him in the Pontiac.

Down the road a ways he said, "Did you leave her the note?"

"I think I forgot it."

"You didn't forget. You just didn't want to do it. I know you, Fanny Gideon, from way, way back."

"I was afraid she'd come and get me. Are you mad with me, Robert?"

"Hell, no, I'm not mad. She deserves what she gets."

"You didn't tell your son."

"I never tell him a thing. Once you start leaving notes it's like asking permission."

She couldn't remember when she had been so happy. "This is like when we were young and ran away to get married." She was smiling at him.

He was smiling too but looking hard at the road. Drivers everywhere were getting crazier all the time. Just stay out of their way. If he lost his license now he wouldn't get it back.

"Robert," she said, "can you remember things?"

"Not as well as I did, but well enough I guess."

"Good," she said. "You take care of the past and I'll handle the present."

"Who's in charge of the future?"

"Oh, it's in charge of itself."

It seemed to him a very funny thing for her to say. "So should we finish what we started back then and get married?" He hadn't planned to say it, but it was said and he was glad.

"What about your wife?"

He tensed to make a turn. "She died."

". . . I'm truly very sorry."

"It's all right," he said. "It's over and done. So do you want to get married?"

"I sort of like the idea of living in sin. Don't you?"

"I do," he said.

At length he put it to her gravely, "If you married me I think they'd leave us alone. We could live somewhere."

"It's too late for that."

"Too late? Like you said, the future is in charge of itself."

A shade passed over her. "I'm too late."

They left the pavement. They drove into the country and now he relaxed. Beside them were fields of greening oats crosshatched with shadows from the passing clouds. Swarms of keening birds swept out of the sky. A whirl of wind whipped out of a tunnel beneath the road. It raked the pasture grasses and combed them all backward and followed the road. The willows in the ditches bridled and dipped.

She tied her sweater loosely in a knot about her throat. "It was raining before. We were driving through rain."

"The windshield misted up. I had to go slow."

"I remember everything about that day." They passed cattle standing knee deep in a lake. "We're running from them now like we did before."

"We're not running from them. Don't think about running. Don't think about them. Think about they're young, with the memories they're proud of crammed with junk, plain junk. There's not much about them we could recommend."

"They're faster," she said. "The people who come after you are always faster. Or they wouldn't win."

He turned into the trees and shifted gears. With a howl from the engine they drove up, up on a pine-needled road. And soon, very soon he pointed to the house tucked away in trees. She exclaimed with delight. There was a series of steps they must climb to reach it. Like a ladder, she laughed. He wanted to help her, but she waved him away. "I've still got my legs." "So you have," he observed her. "You're like a mountain goat. I've gotten slower."

Inside was a small and airless room with a hearth at one end and a bed at the other. There was a smell of ash. Against one wall was a rusting stove. "I told you not fancy."

"I didn't come for fancy." It made her think of an acorn, brown and secret, the way a room should be that lives in trees. She could feel the swaying of her childhood treehouse when the wind blew at dusk and she pulled her long hair over her head to match the birds snug in their rippling feathers.

"It's got a bathroom off that door by the bed."

"And a porch," she whispered, knowing it was there on the other side of another door. She pulled it open and walked out slowly. The sun was nesting in a giant maple full of summer. The lowest branches swept the weathered boards. The massive trunk fell out of sight below. She dropped her purse and settled like a wren among the leaves.

He watched her from the doorway. Then he joined her, stepping through the branches to inspect what lay beneath. The floor of the forest dropped sharply away. The porch had the look of being blown into the hillside and the house that followed it propped on piles. Fanny's own treehouse had been better made.

He returned to her and stood among the mammoth branches, their leaf clusters hanging like fruit in the motionless air. He smiled at her but he could not speak. He had lost the power and the spell of a tree, lost how it was to feel himself all gone into the green . . . to desire it so much . . . to climb anything, to swing from anything, a rope, a vine, daring death to get it . . . a craving so strong it was strange it wasn't called immoral or illegal. But then the moralists were all grown up. He had been young and full of the craving and Fanny Gideon had given him her tree. If she hadn't had a treehouse, would they have loved?

She looked up at him with happiness. "We have always been married."

He held out his hand. She pulled it down and kissed it and kept it in hers. "Your hand is just the way I need a hand to be. Not young and not old. Take care of it," she said.

"I will," he said, moved, and knowing he would have loved her without her tree. "Are you hungry?" he asked. "There might be something in there."

She shook her head. "I'm too happy to eat. This is the happiest I've ever been. I've forgotten the rest."

Her happiness began to make him afraid. Like the tree before them, it was larger than life. There was nothing to tell him if it was real, or if she had made it to hide her fear. Her fear was real, for he felt it stir in the deep of his throat, in the palm of his hand, the way he would know whatever was wrong when she was a girl. When they climbed the ladder it was always there for the tree to know. For him to know if he knew the tree. He had learned the tree. On the calmest day he could feel it wanting to circle and toss, have some fun, give them something to think about. On a windy day he would spin with it, going green inside, getting into its marrow, feeling within it the way she was, knowing he would marry the way she was, the way he felt the way she was . . . And now he was troubled with the empty years. They turned in his bones where they must have lain but he hadn't known. What he dreaded most at this time of his life was to live through anything over again. The flight they'd begun being ended again, the door they had opened being shut once more. Life had come to seem like a series of things that repeated themselves, until one day he had closed his heart. It was better perhaps to forget . . . like Fanny. He could feel something break like a bough in the woods.

Her eyes had never left the tree. The air was stirring. A shudder swept through the leaves and into her. "How long will we be here?"

"Till we want to leave."

"Till they find us, you mean?"

He did not reply. He was aware that the tree was growing dark within. Only the tips of branches were still green-gold. Somewhere deep within it was a whir of wings. He went inside and found some coffee to brew in a pan. There were crackers in a tin, but they seemed too stale. He came out with her coffee. "It's the best we have."

She took the cup absently and drank a little. "It's very good, Robert." She laid the cup on the floor. Her voice, it seemed to him, was just as it had been. In the failing light he saw her face again young and kindling the treehouse they had never let go. Her hair was the color it had been in the moonlight . . .

He found a weathered chair that had been tipped against the wall. He drew it across the floor and sat beside her in the dusk. It was dark in the tree. They could hear the birds within settling into the night, and somewhere an owl. And a wind came from nowhere to sleep in the woods, bedding down in the leaves but restless, turning, sighing, troubled with dreams, sleepwalking in leaf mold, crouching in the chimney, falling into the ravine . . . It was turning cooler. "Where is the moon?" she asked with longing in her voice.

"It isn't time, Mrs. Moonlight. Give it time." He stroked her hair while they sat between the tree dark and the dark of their room, between two darks with an equal claim, and neither would release them into the other. But fireflies wove the darks into night . . . He took her hand and led her, it seemed to her, into the tree, but it must have been the room. For she lay on the bed and he took off her glasses and then her shoes. He covered her with a blanket that smelled of smoke.

"I want you near me," she said.

So he lay down beside her. "There isn't a light," he whispered. "Do you mind the dark?"

"Not when you are with me."

He found her hands and kissed them. They were trembling and cold. He drew the blanket closely about her throat.

She said, "I won't think about anything but now. Or remember . . . I won't remember anything but then. I fight all the time to keep from losing myself. They try to make me remember the things they want me to remember. Why do I have to remember *their* things? Never mine. My things. Go to a nursing home because I left my coat in the park? Such a fuss she made. I didn't care about the coat. I never liked it. I didn't try to remember it. I don't have room in my mind for all the things they want me to remember. I just have room for when you kissed me in the treehouse . . . and I was Mrs. Moonlight. It fills up my brain. There's no room for the rest."

"Don't think about the rest." He kissed her hair.

"I have to think of it. I have to," she said.

He could feel that she was losing all the joy of the tree, as if the wind they heard were blowing it away and blowing her with it away from him. "Don't think," he begged her.

"I have to think of it," she said. He could feel her pain. "When she tore down the treehouse it was like she tore me down. Like she tore down the things of mine I need to remember. I can't forgive her for that. And now I want to forget her . . . along with the rest. She will put me in that home so I might as well forget her . . . Help me do it," she said. She was weeping now. "Help me forget her and just remember you."

He held her face in his hands. "I would if I could but I don't know how. I have never known how." He took his hands away. His mind was heavy with the chirring of the crickets round their bed. Birds had flown in and were muttering in the gloom above the open door. After a time he said through her weeping, as if to himself. "Whiskey is a good thing but it doesn't last. I tried it for a while when my wife stopped loving me . . . It doesn't last."

"I need something to last."

"I know," he said. "I know. But it always comes back. I closed myself up for most of my life. Till today when you called . . ."

She turned to embrace him. "You will be always in my mind. All the rest will go but you. Do you believe it?" she said.

"I believe it, Mrs. Moonlight. I truly do."

She lay quietly beside him, sleeping a little, waking to find him sleeping, then waking again to find him waking too. A full moon had risen behind the tree. The churning leaves were frothing the light that struck the bed. "I'm trying to forget her. It's hard, so hard. It's like your own children get stuck in your mind. Maybe when they're born to you they aren't all born. Maybe a part of them is left inside . . . Hold me," she said.

He folded his arms about her.

"When you hold me I can almost . . . There's so much . . . so much. She would run and always open her little hands to fall. They were full of stone bruises and splinters and cuts . . . I would look at her hands and I'd kiss them and cry . . ."

"Try to sleep," he said.

"Red flowers made her smile . . ." It was a while before she asked, "Do you think they'll come?"

"My son is smart enough to figure this out."

"But not before morning?"

He felt the brush of a moth upon his lips. "Not before then."

"So we have tonight. We mustn't fall asleep."

But they did. When he woke she was gone. He sat up in panic. His fear was so strong his heart was beating in his throat. He could not hear a sound but the wind in the tree. Suppose she had forgotten where she was and fallen down the steps or walked into the woods and fallen into the ravine . . .

He stumbled to the porch, where he found her in the moonlight among the moving leaves. He did not trust his voice to speak. He drew her up to him and held her. She was as soft as a girl. As small as she had been. As yielding as then.

"Robert?" she said. "Robert?" Her voice was breaking with bewilderment. "Why are we here?" She pulled away from his arms. "This isn't our treehouse. Who does it belong to? My daughter tore it down . . . the one I had made. Why are we here?" she said again. "Are we running away?"

"There's no reason," he said. "Come inside," he begged.

"Don't let them take us back."

"No," he whispered. "No."

She caught her breath. "I forget . . . But the old things are there." She reached a hand to the tree. "New things that happen are so hard to keep. They fall through the leaves . . . Unless they break your heart. Unless they're what she did." She turned to search his face. "How did we get here? There's a room . . . and a bed."

"Yes, inside. Come inside."

"There's one way," she said.

"Tell me," he said, hardly hearing her words. She was trembling in his arms.

"Then I have to tell you this one thing you never knew. After they brought us back, they tore down our treehouse."

"I knew that," he said. "I went to see it one night and it was gone."

"But you didn't know that after that I tried to kill myself. I was crazy with grief. I didn't want to live. I cut my wrist. I wanted that much to die. When you're fifteen you're crazy like a fox, they said. I was ashamed of it later."

After a moment she pulled back her sleeve and showed him the scar. He found it in the moonlight and kissed it slowly.

"What if they hadn't found me and made me live?"

"What are you saying?"

"I want to go back and die to the rest of my life. I want to go back and die before my daughter came."

"But you went on living."

"What if I hadn't?"

"Then what are we now tonight?" he asked in despair.

"This is another life. Don't you feel it?" she said.

"You're saying it isn't real?"

"Oh, no, it's the realest thing that's ever been."

He was stroking her hair. "Your hair is like moonlight . . . Come back to bed."

He led her inside and they lay down together, side by side, hands touching, eyes closed against the dark. "I love you, Mrs. Moonlight." He heard her breath growing faint. "Please don't die," he pled. Her hair was like smoke. He drew the smoke of their blanket to cover them both.

"No, I'm only going backward. A part of me will die." She was weeping. They wept together. He held her in his arms.

"Don't go to sleep," she said. "I need you to help me."

"I don't know how," he wept. "I don't know what you're doing."

"I'm making it that she never happened to me."

"Are you sure it's what you want?"

"Yes, I am. I'm sure. You're the only one ever that belonged in my life . . . Think about the way we were. Think about the moon."

He could hear the owl. Beyond her hair, through the door he could see how the wind was slicing the moonlight, tossing it with leaves, thrusting it deep . . . and deeper into the tree. "You never let me kiss you but once a day, even though we said that we were going to be married. You were that shy."

"I'm not now," she said. "Kiss me now."

He kissed her long and gently, like an echo of the way it used to be. And the way it used to be reechoed till at last she was hearing nothing else, not the wind in the leaves, not the owl, not her daughter's voice . . . After a time she whispered, "It all slips away unless I hold on. It's like I am singing and the words blow away."

"Marry me," he said, "and I'll remember for you." Beneath his hand her head was tracing a refusal. "Everything you need to keep I'll keep for you."

"There's just a little bit and I can keep it myself and let go the rest."

He was losing his breath in the smoke of her hair. "If you do she'll put you in the home all the sooner."

"I know it," she said. "But this way it will be like a stranger has done it. Nothing a stranger does to you can make any difference."

It was morning when they woke to a thrasher's song. Beyond the door the tree was like another country in another season. It glistened. It unfolded. Light and shadow flew about in it like restless birds.

They heard the car outside. He rose and went to the window. "Well, they're here," he said. "It's my son's gray car."

Then her daughter entered, hair disheveled, eyes wild with reproach. "Mama, why have you done this? Why are you here?"

Fanny Gideon looked up at her serenely. "Do I know you?" she said.

The birdsong throbbed in the maple tree and circled the bed where Fanny Gideon lay with her hair on the pillow like a bridal veil. Her daughter turned upon him her shocked, accusing face. "How dare you take her?"

Long ago, when he was still a boy who swung from trees, before she was born, someone who was like her had asked him the same. It seemed to him that now he had grown into the answer. He summoned all his force to make a stand against her and against all the ones who ride you down to take you back and stash you in some corner, flush you down some snakehole, throw you away.

"Not this time," he said to her, calling up the memory of that ancient flight and capture. "This time we're married."

He saw her face give way . . . He found Fanny's glasses and put them on her.

She sat up in bed and looked past the strange woman standing beside her. The tree itself seemed to sing with the bird. She had only to rise to belong to the tree world, belong to its mystery, the mystery of greenness, her own sweet youth. She smiled at him, seeing him deep in the green, seeing him already shadowed with leaves. On this first morning of the rest of their life she remembered him. As she always would.

The Light on the Water

She painted watercolors of the sea. Anything that could be finished in a day, but mostly sea. It was plainly in the faces of all who were around her that this, or any day, might be the last that was given. The light upon the water would brighten and fail. When it brightened again, she might not be there to see. When Vito, the Sicilian gardener, planted bulbs in spring and fall, it was in his rueful whistle, in the way he slipped them with a furtive, leathered hand into the earth, that he planted them for others, not herself, to enjoy. Or she would come upon his children blooming in the sun like seeds he had scattered, eight of them with eyes as black as berries, drinking water from the birdbath, their noses gold with pollen from the flowers they had sniffed, and they would hush at once, as if they had been warned their voices could bring her days to an end. She did not like to see them, for children were denied her. But her gaze would come to rest on Vito's father, small and sinewy like his son. He sometimes waited with a cane at the garden gate. He had been himself a gardener till his eyes had failed. How beautiful he was . . . how lucky to be old.

She felt a deep and quiet urgency to make a single day complete in itself. The picture finished. The paints and brushes put away. The slow walk through the garden. An hour's rest. The mail opened, each letter answered at once. A prelude on her spinet, something soft but not searching. Supper with her husband Eric, home for the night. Then bed and her simple prayer to be granted another day. She never turned out the light; she was afraid of the dark.

Sometimes there would be friends who dropped in for tea. Just a few. Not for long. Her father might come to sit and smooth her dark hair as he had when she was young. He had taken to carving wood for want of a better thing to do, and the roughness of his hand would slightly tangle her hair. But his eyes were full of tenderness. He called her his princess. Everyone treated Beth as if she were young and were exempted from the cares and obligations that might otherwise pertain to her thirty-eight years. Indeed, since her illness she had forgotten such things. She had turned away as well from joy and grief, from desire and loss, lest her ailing heart be seared by them and fail to beat.

Marian, her friend from school days, would drop by after tennis, her arms bronzed, her face blooming with health. Marian had had an early marriage that failed. She told Beth it didn't matter. It was all for the best. "I wasn't ready," she said, stroking her beautiful arms.

"Are you now?" Beth smiled. She liked the glowing energy that tried to be contained in the presence of herself but that smoldered in the body like a warm sweet incense and broke away at last to drift in the room.

Marian only smiled into the roses on the table.

One afternoon Eric came home early and Marian was there. He entered the room without warning. Beth saw the look between them. Energies visible for the moment had met before her eyes, and clothed in supple flesh had met in secret before. It was unmistakable. She saw it with a shock she would not let herself feel. Instead, it sank downward like a stone into a pool, and she knew it cold and hard at the bottom of her heart.

And there was no one to tell. The hard, cold stone was a threat to her life unless she could reveal it to someone else, someone who would share with her the alien thing. Her father would only stroke her hair a little longer.

She put off calling Peter Kilbourne, but in the end she did. She had met him one summer at the lake in Maine. He was older, years older, with hair an ashen gray. His face had an almost Oriental look. The skin was smooth and tight, and beneath the summer tan it was slightly amber. He had a fragile, brittle leanness, as if he had been scissored out of fine gold leaf. His eyes were soft shadows in fields of gold. They were richly kind. He had rented a cottage several doors from theirs.

They met in a copse of birches overlooking the lake while Eric and her father were hiking in the hills. She was there with her watercolors, trying once again to catch the light on the water. And he had come up to tell her she was good, very good, but if she wanted light and water she should go to the lakes that were high up in the hills. "I know nothing myself, being only a writer. But my friend is a painter and he says it is the thing . . . I could drive you," he said.

She shook her head. "The altitude is bad for me. My heart is weak."

"How weak?" he said gravely.

She laid her brush down to answer. "Weak enough to love the sun every morning."

"I know the feeling," he said.

She looked at him with a question in her eyes. But, meeting his own, she did not have to ask it. They shared a way of living.

"Mine is something else," he said, dismissing it.

After that there was a substance like a tender spot of flesh that each protected for the other. There were no words to express it. She did not try. Once in October she had driven with her father into Boston, where he wanted to see some wood carvings on display. She waited in the park in the leaf-bright autumn with her book in her hand. And suddenly she was looking into the smile of Peter Kilbourne. And his smile said: We made it. We had the sun this morning . . .

He seemed older and frailer as he stood in yellow leaves looking down at her, his face an autumn color like the leaves at his feet. He said, "You're very much like an actress I loved when I was young. A lovely woman with sweet dreaming eyes and hair a dark cloud. But she wore it up a little more as I recall. It was the fashion then . . . When I read she was dying I went out and walked into the path of a car."

"On purpose?" she asked.

"I never knew . . . I think I may have thought that I could buy her life with mine."

She smiled at him thoughtfully.

"I never met her," he said. He sat beside her on the bench. "I met you instead."

She looked off into the trees. "Am I dying too?" she asked.

"We all are in the end. I've come to find it a very comforting thought. But I shall see that you live a long and wonderful life."

He was full of things like that; she wasn't meant to understand. Or so she had decided.

"I live nearby," he told her. He wrote down his address in the back of her book. "Come by if you can. If you ever need me, call . . ." And he wrote down his number.

Now she called him for the first time because her need was great. Inside she was a clenched fist that would not open to pain, and she told him a little about the light on the sea, the way it was in early spring. She was painting it, she said. But he read her too well. He heard the dark in her voice. He did not ask what it was. "Why don't you visit me?" he said. She knew that she had called to hear him say the words.

There was Meg, who lived in Boston and owned a decorating shop. She had known Meg for years. She told Eric she would visit her. He was doubtful about the trip.

"But I've done this before. Meg will meet the plane."

As they spoke of her departure, she was seeing them together, her husband and her friend: I make it easy for them. But then she had the intuition that instead she made it hard . . . that they thrived on stolen moments, that time given freely, long hours and days, would not be to their purpose. She did not know why.

She phoned Eric from the hotel. She said she was with Meg. Then she called Meg. "I hate to do this, but I'm in Boston and Eric thinks I'm with you. Could you cover for me if he calls?" With her father and with Eric she had long since grown accustomed to the smaller deceptions. Pretending she wasn't tired. Pretending she had taken a taxi, not the bus. Pretending she had slept . . .

She could hear Meg's silence. "Sure I will . . . You want to tell me where you'll be? Look, honey, I'm not into your business, but you're not all that well . . ."

She sighed. "Of course. I'll be visiting with a writer I met at the lake, called Peter Kilbourne. He's in the phone book . . . and he's rather old, Meg."

"As long as there's breath," Meg observed.

"I'll be around to see you later on and spend the night."

"Anytime."

She lay down for an hour. When she rang Peter's bell, to her surprise a nurse answered. "What is it?" Beth said quickly, stifling her alarm.

The other, crisp and pigeon breasted, drew her reedy lips into a fragment of a smile and led her back to his bedroom and left her there.

Through the one long window came a winter-thin light. It fell across the bed, where he lay among white pillows that made his yellow pallor even more pronounced. His hair had gone white. She was startled to see how very ill he looked. But his voice was just as it had been, a little frailer but glad. "Come in, my dear."

"I shouldn't have come. I didn't know . . ."

He broke in upon her. "Come close. I want to see you. And I'm not all that sick. They tell me to lie here and it's easier to do it than to put up a fight. That woman you encountered is terribly strong. I like to keep her on my side."

She helped him to sit up with pillows at his back. He seemed happy to have her. "I knew you would come. Sooner or later. Would you turn on the lamp so I can see you better?"

She sat beside him in the pool of amber light. He told her of his health, but she had the impression that his illness had long since ceased to interest him, that he was telling her in order to make a little space in which she could rest before she told him of her trouble.

"You always remind me of that woman I loved. Maria Brittain was her name. She was before your day. A wonderful actress. All fire and ice."

She smiled at him thinly. "I can manage the ice."

"Has something changed?" he said at last.

"No," she said with calm sadness. "Nothing ever changes. Everyone sees that nothing changes for me. It's just that I slowly become aware of things."

"A disturbing thing?" he said, to help her. "Tell me only if you wish."

"I wish," she said, "that you could look into my mind and see it all there without my telling you."

"Eric?" he said at last.

Her silence confirmed it. "It's the light on the water. You look away to dip your brush in the paint and it's changed when you look back . . . It was changing all along, but you didn't see until you looked away."

"And so you looked away and when you looked back your life with Eric was changed."

"She has been there all along."

"I see," he said.

"I cannot blame him," she said. "Dear God, I cannot blame him . . . When he holds me, I school myself to feel nothing of his embrace, and he knows it and accepts it. But it isn't enough. Not for him. And not for me." She steeled herself into composure. "I am given a life but I mustn't live it." Her voice was very low; tears were coursing down her cheeks. "If I live it I die."

"My dear lady of Shalott," he said with deep compassion and looked away. He waited for her. Presently he recited softly, " 'She has heard a whisper say . . .' " His eyes scanned the window, where he seemed to find the lines: " 'A curse is on her if she stay/ To look down to Camelot.' Forgive me for seeking words. There are no words. Except 'sorrow' and 'pain.' "

She drew her breath slowly. "I sometimes think that when I die it will not be the same as it is for others, however that may be . . . Death will hardly be a change from the life I have." She brushed away her tears. Her voice was desolate. "I cannot let myself feel the pain of my loss. How wonderful it must be to give in to grief. To feel every drop of the sorrow that is there."

"He will leave?" he said.

"Oh, no. Oh, no. He will stay because I mustn't . . ." She dared not go on. "It is very hard."

"Perhaps he doesn't want to leave. Perhaps he only wants what you cannot give."

"What I cannot give? I can give him nothing. Not a child. Not love . . ."

She lapsed into silence. The clock beside his bed was ticking in a whisper. He reached a thin yellowed hand for a glass of pink liquid on the table by his bed and sipped it slowly. "My dear, you must forgive me. May I ring for some tea? She makes it. Not well, but it's faintly reminiscent of a cup of tea."

She shook her head. "Nothing." She glanced at the clock. "I've stayed much too long. I mustn't tire you." But she could not leave.

"And I mustn't tire you. But we're not tiring one another. We never have. You mustn't leave until you've heard what you came to hear."

She did not understand.

"Although you didn't know it, you came all this way so I could tell you something that you need to know . . . I have waited for you. I was beginning to think you wouldn't come in time."

She sighed. "You always talk to me in riddles."

"I want you to listen very carefully."

She looked at him gravely. "I always have."

He was holding the glass. He looked into it for a moment, swirling the liquid, then returned it to the table. "My doctors don't give me a lot of time," he said.

"Don't leave," she said softly.

"It will come." He was gentle with her. "But I'm leaving you something."

"Oh, my dear, I need nothing. What I need is you."

"I'm not leaving you money." He was almost impatient. "I'm leaving you something that is far more precious. I'm leaving you the life you deserve to have."

She simply looked at him. His words were meaningless to her.

"There is a way," he said, "and I can do it for you. I have read of it, studied it. I've been involved in it with others. The painter friend I spoke of . . . It has a name, though perhaps you haven't heard it. It's called the practice of substitution and exchange."

She shook her head. "I don't know what you mean."

"I mean that my liver in the end will get the best of me. It's a matter of time. Not much at that. Why should I die of a liver disease when I might as well die of something else? What difference does it make how you go when you go?"

"What are you saying?"

The nurse was standing in the doorway. He waved her away. "I'm saying that I might as well go with my heart."

"But your heart is sound?" She put it as a question. She was certain now of nothing.

"So I'm told. But your illness of the heart I shall take upon myself. And when I have done this you will be freed of it. You will be well." His kind, grave eyes were asking her to hear his words and take his gift.

"This is not possible," she said softly in amazement.

"Believe me, it is."

"And if it were possible, I couldn't accept it."

"Why not?" he countered gaily. "It might as well be my heart as my liver. Besides, I'm going to do it anyway."

She could almost laugh. "It's not possible," she said. "It can't be done."

"But you know nothing of it." His face had taken on an animation. "It's an ancient doctrine. The ancients knew it. The Greeks and later. And today. You'd be surprised how many. I could give you books but they'd bore you. Sometimes in the practice there is a kind of exchange. Exchange of one another's burdens, whatever they may be. A glorious thing indeed . . . But you and I, my dear, won't do anything so fancy. Between us there will be a little substitution. To state it simply, and it is a simple thing, I shall take your place in your illness. I shall accept it . . . undergo it. All you need is faith that I can do it for you."

She laughed at him gently and lovingly. "You've very sweet . . ."

"But you can't have the faith . . . Well, it's not essential. It would make the waiting easier. I have planned from the first to do it for you. But I've told you today to make the present moment a better thing. The present is hard for you."

The clock was muttering her pain. She looked down at her hands and then into his yellowed parchment face. "You're beautiful," she said. "Have I told you that? You're so good for me. I can be with you and not feel I ought to be . . . something more."

He shook his head. "You mustn't turn away from my words."

"You scarcely know me," she said, wondering. "And because of that lady of yours long ago . . ."

"It's not because of her, or only a little because I let her die. But then I was going about it all wrong . . ." He smiled at her then. "Scarcely know you!" he exclaimed. "I have known you all this life. I may have known you in another. I know you better than you know yourself. Can't you tell?"

She could believe that he did. And how was the mystery. But as for what he proposed . . .

"Wait and see, my lady of Shalott," he said. "Have a wonderful time in Camelot. And while you're having it think of me."

It was May when she happened to hear of his death. For a week she had felt unusually well. She had finished her picture and put away her paints. And she sat in the garden with her face in the sun. On the tray Rosa brought her a letter from Meg with the sandwich for lunch, a glass of milk, and the little blue pill. She ate the sandwich and drank the milk. On an impulse she threw the pill into the marigolds. How childish, she thought, and yet she smiled. With the sun on her face she stroked the letter. Then she tore it open. Meg had written: "You remember that writer you went to see—Peter Kilbourne? The morning's paper said he died. If you haven't heard, I thought you'd want to know."

Beth sat with the words, repressing at once the stab of sorrow. She had written him a letter, which he had not answered. She had written another. The visit came back with great clarity. She found herself reaching for the things he had said. Precisely his words. She recalled he had spoken of Camelot.

She could hear the bees humming in the beds of iris. A breeze was bringing her the smell of the sea. She went inside to call Meg's number. "What did the paper say he died off? Peter Kilbourne."

"I don't remember. I think it said . . . I hope Dan hasn't thrown the thing away. Can you hold? Here it is. It says . . ." She stopped, remembering Beth's heart. "I thought you told me he had a liver thing. They may have it wrong, but it says heart failure."

"They may have it wrong," Beth echoed her.

After that she sat for a while in the sun. Then she stood up slowly, as the doctor had instructed her always to do. She walked to the end of the garden and back. The ground moss was damp. The air scented with pine was uncommonly fresh. She could hear Vito's children in the garden shed . . . She began very slowly to walk again. She opened the side gate and went down the street. There were pools of shining water from the night before. In her thin canvas shoes she walked straight through them into yesterday's rain. A line of young birches was radiant with light. Beneath them she was moving through shadows of leaves. She could feel moving shadows of leaves on her face. Then leaves were moving in her, in her throat, her arms, her breasts. She walked faster and faster. A little boy with a red pail left his yard and followed. She heard the sound of his running. Suddenly she turned and took the child in her arms.

She said nothing of this. After a week she called the doctor's office. Her regular appointment was two weeks away, but now she asked for an immediate date. Vito drove her as he always did, gripping the wheel with a sinewy hand that was caked with earth. The other badgered the radio for music to soothe her ailing heart. He filled the car with the smell of loam. Once there, on an impulse she took the stairs. On the final flight she began to run.

The doctor was one she had had for years. He was swarthy, precise, with a cast in his eye. He always seemed to be looking to the left of her. He listened to her heart and charted its beats. "You must have been following all my instructions. Taking it easy. That's very good."

"No," she told him, "I ran up the stairs."

"Did you!" he smiled, looking off to her side. "That wouldn't be wise."

"Just now," she said. "Ten minutes ago."

He patted her shoulder. He did not believe her. "You're doing exceptionally well," he said. "I think we'll continue the little blue pills."

"How well is exceptionally well?" she asked.

He listened again to her heart for a while. Then he crammed his stethoscope into his pocket. "Well, at this moment, if I didn't know better, I'd say you had a perfectly normal heart. But of course I know better. And to rely upon an occasional reading that's good would be unwise. In your type of trouble there is no remission."

Eric was reading the news on the porch. He was in his green slacks and ready for tennis. Perhaps with Marian. She would not ask. She was thinking how very beautiful he was. He was ten years older but he might have been ten years younger than she, with his boyish face and sweep of copper hair and his limbs that seemed to be waiting for motion, his skin that seemed to be holding light.

"I didn't hear the car." He had not looked up.

"I walked," she said. "I didn't wait for Vito."

He looked up then. "Not far, I hope." He scanned her face with his blue eyes that never quite took her in and turned to his paper.

She did not answer. She gazed at him with all the love she had denied herself. She felt his arms around her, his mouth on her throat, his breath in her hair. Her response was so great that she could not stand.

She sat before him and began to weep with joy and grief. Her grief was for the joy that came too late. The familiar look of masked alarm came into his eyes.

"It's all right," she said, her eyes streaming tears. "My heart is well."

He smiled. "You had a good report? That's no reason to cry."

"Not a good report. I'm really well."

But he could not comprehend her words. Her illness was too much a part of their life. After eighteen years he would not know her without it, and now it seemed he did not want her without it. For later on, when he had said goodnight, she came to his bed, where she had not been for months. She lay beside him and pulled his face against her breast. He kissed her gently on throat and cheek. "Love me, Eric," she whispered.

He held her briefly. "You've had enough for today. The trip to town. And you walked. I wish you hadn't walked."

"I'm well. My heart is well."

"I'm so glad," he said and rose and led her to her own bed. He kissed both her hands and covered her gently. "Did you take your blue pill?"

The following morning when she came to breakfast he looked up from his eggs with a mild surprise. "Rosa will be up with it in a minute."

"I'm coming to breakfast from now on," she said.

"There's no reason."

"There is a reason. I'm well."

She had the feeling that he found her insistence on her wellness like that of a child who wants to go out to play in spite of a fever.

In the days to come she grew aware that those around her had subtly and safely imprisoned her in illness, and now it would be unsettling to set her free. Her father. Even Rosa, who insisted on trays for breakfast and lunch. Her relentless reminders: "You better lie down now . . ." "You ain't took your pill." And Vito, who disappeared when she entered the garden, as if she were a spirit who must haunt it in peace . . . or if she should die there, die in peace. His children watched her, as motionless as stones, from the branches of trees; they scattered when she called, as if they feared contagion. Once she heard them say, "The sick lady will hear . . ." With Eric, there was Marian and something between them that was made of her illness. She tried to understand what it was.

To be given the whole of Camelot and never allowed to walk abroad . . . Then the gift of her life was thrown away. They must have perceived that she no longer tired, that she walked for hours, that she swam in the sea. But none of this did their faces mirror. They seemed to regard the change in her as a kind of perverseness they must endure. Still she lived in the dream they had dreamt for her.

At last she persuaded them to let her travel alone to Maine. With visible misgivings they reserved her a room. She sat by the lake in the warm, sweet days and tried to recover a world she had lost. In the mornings the deer would come down to drink. As she watched, the blue water flooded her throat. In her mind she followed them into the wood till at last she emerged on the farther side to walk in the hills beside other lakes and wait for the deer that came down to drink. And these were the lakes Peter gave to her, the ones he had wanted her once to have, the ones she had been afraid to have. The light on their water was more than fair and all he could ever wish for her.

Even here she was living a dream, Peter's dream. And yet he would want for her more than dream . . . She could not help missing her father and Eric and the children that stared at her from the trees. She was thirty-eight and she had no child. It came to her as she sat by the lake in Peter's dream that a child would free her from all their dreams and give her a life that she could live.

Eric called one night. "You left your paints. Shall I run them up?"

"I don't want to paint . . . I want a child."

She heard his silence. "Is the weather good?"

She said in despair, oblivious of listeners that perched like sparrows on the party line, "I know about Marian. I've been given my life. I'm giving you yours."

His voice broke with alarm. "Could we discuss this another time?"

"I'm setting you free."

"Goodbye," he said.

When she returned, her fair skin tanned, her dark hair tangled with bits of fern, he made no reference at all to her words. She told her father as he smoothed her hair. He was bitterly opposed to freedom of the sort. "But he loves someone else."

"I don't care about that. He promised to keep you in sickness and health. Things can change and the vow takes care of that."

It was clear that he had no faith in her health.

More than ever before their care imprisoned her. They needed her illness. Her father, alone since her mother's death, needed the child that it now provided. And Eric and Marian needed her illness. Her insufficiencies as a wife had provided the pardon for what they enjoyed. In some chamber of her mind she dwelt with the knowledge. She must be their victim and at once their atonement. She saw how it haunted the eyes of the lovers, who were never at ease. The change in her threatened their peace of mind. She knew it in Eric's brief atoning kiss. She knew it in Marian's gifts of expiation—the silken scarf, the sandalwood soap, the hour stolen from tennis. There were more of them since her return from the lake.

Her mended health fostered a further awareness, for all her perceptions were heightened now: their passion, however clothed in supple flesh, surprisingly was not of itself enough. It needed concealment, the excitement of stealth. They burrowed like moles. She would come upon the telltale rise in the earth. The toast in the eyes to a memory they shared when with one accord they raised their cups of tea . . . or the kiss Marian left on the rim of her glass, which Eric brushed with his lips when he took it away . . . or, after her visit, the words subtly marked in the evening news for Eric later to find . . . They must have it so. And thus they declined the freedom she offered. She was helpless to break a pattern so durable. It had been years in the making.

And for years they had nurtured the child in her. She found herself rebelling in childish ways. She would go for the day without leaving them word, and then return late to cause them concern. She would walk by the sea in the dark of the night when the waves were high. In the end she restored their peace of mind. With a tender precision they balanced betrayal with an anxious care. In the scales of their justice, the graver their worry, the keener the pleasures they stole for themselves.

Now they seemed to arrange to meet in her presence. While she sat with Marian in the garden, Eric came. She felt at once how they savored her nearness, how it sharpened desire. Like the bright summer day she was part of their hunger. She sat between them in the perfumed air with a droning of bees. When the two grew silent, she could all but taste the honey of their pleasure, fashioned of flowers and cunning and guilt. They warmed to her because she enhanced their joy. They watched the bees wallowing in the yellow roses . . . There was a stone in her breast.

Once she came upon Vito in the arbor. He was high on the ladder tying the grapes. Without knowing why, she paced beneath him. Perhaps because he was free of her world and dwelt with the earth and sun and air. She felt how she trapped him there in the vines, how he longed to escape as he always had. And as she paced she began to cry. She was crying because they both were trapped. It was good to allow herself to weep. She was glad that Vito could see her tears.

"Vito . . . where are your children today?" she called to him in a broken voice.

He was so distressed he could scarcely speak. "I keep them from here. They make you noise." She could tell he thought she would die at last.

"No, no, they must come. You must let them come. They make me glad."

But it wasn't so. Nothing made her glad.

One day, without telling them, she took a boat that stopped for the day at a tiny island. It had a windmill to look at and fishermen to watch as they flung out their lines along a rotting wharf. Inside the little shop at the base of the windmill she had tea and toast and listened to herons. Then she walked beside the water as she did at home, wondering why she had come when it was so much the same. The sky and the sea were a silver gray.

She came upon a man in a small straw hat. He was painting the water. She watched at some distance. It was as if she were watching herself. He looked back at her finally with a look that told her he had known she was there.

"Hello," he said.

She came close. He was younger than she. She could not say why he reminded her of Peter. Perhaps it was his leanness. Or his gentle, golden eyes.

"Do you paint?" he said affably.

"I used to," she said.

"Water is hard to do. Did you ever try water?"

She nodded. "I never got the light."

"God, it changes," he said.

He went on with his painting. It was oils he was doing. "What made you stop?" he asked finally.

"My life changed."

"Like the water?"

"Something like that . . . Good luck," she added and walked away down the beach. She was circling the island.

After a while she looked up and he was coming toward her with his painting gear beneath his arms. He said, "I knew if I walked away from you our circles would meet . . . Would you call that following?"

She smiled. "I don't know." But she knew it was something that Peter might have said. And a circling was in her, as of a gull before it falls.

"Would you care to sit with me beneath these scrubby trees? We could talk about our lives or the water or the light."

She looked at him, speckled as a hen with his paints. The grays he had mixed for the pearl of this sea. The yellows and whites for a sunnier day. The greens for shadows where the waves had tipped. She heard herself: "I mustn't miss the boat." Far away on the wharf the other passengers were walking between the lines of fishermen.

He looked at his watch, which was stippled with green. "We have time for your life. I think mine is too long."

They walked to where the sand invaded the scrub. He stashed all his gear against a tree. They sat down in the shade. A small boat was bobbing far out on the water. A seagull dipped.

"I don't want to talk about my life," she said.

"Lives are boring," he admitted. He smelled richly of paint.

She picked up a curled shell and shook it free of sand. She put it to her ear and she heard the distant waves like a pounding heart. "There's a thing I've wanted to ask someone. Have you heard of something called substitution and exchange?"

"Tell me about it."

"I don't understand it."

He turned and kissed her gently. Nothing about his lips reminded her of Eric's. It was totally a new thing. Very new on her lips.

"Is it important to you?" he said.

"It is very important." She looked out to sea with the shell to her ear. "It's a matter of life and death."

"Then I should be told."

"You're like someone," she whispered, "that I used to know."

"Did you love him?"

"Yes, I loved him."

He kissed her hands, first the one with the shell. She longed to kiss his. If she stayed she would kiss them. She rose and walked away.

He stood looking after her. "Would you tell me tomorrow? I'll be here all day."

All that night she dreamt of lying with him in the sand. And all the next day the island burned into her mind. She had saved the curled shell; when she held it to her ear, she heard the beat of her heart. The laughter of Vito's children was near. They were drinking the water for the birds again.

Eric returned for supper and frowned into his food. "I've been waiting for you to tell me where you went yesterday. I kept calling, you know."

She did not answer him. Instead she said, "You must give me a child . . . or I shall get someone else."

He stared at her as if she had gone out of her mind. "You're not strong enough. And even if you were, it's too late."

"Too late?"

"You're too old."

She could not speak for the sorrow that gripped her breast, and then for the rage that took its place.

The following morning she sat alone by the sea and remembered the island. She glanced at her watch and saw that the boat would be landing soon. The windmill was visible. The fishermen on the wharf were tossing their lines. The passengers were scattering. And in the distance was the solitary figure with his canvas and paints. She was walking toward him in her canvas shoes that were filling with sand. And he glanced up to say, "Have you come to tell me?" She looked at him with love. "I've come to show you." She hardly knew what she meant.

When the letters came, there was one from Meg. It was about Peter Kilbourne. "I was in the library and someone brought his book back while I was there. When I saw his name I couldn't resist asking, 'Oh, did you like it?' It was a woman who said she was a niece of his. She said she guessed I would wonder why she hadn't bought it. She said she borrowed them first and then if she liked them she went out and bought them. She said he thought it was a great idea. Even I could tell she was too cheap to buy her own uncle's book and wouldn't buy this one though she said she liked it. 'By the way, how did he die?' I said. 'Well, he had this liver disease,' she said. There was nothing anyone could do, she said. She said it was a very fatal condition. I'm trying to imagine if very fatal is any quicker than fatal. But I'm not undercutting the sadness of it. I mentioned that the paper said it was heart. But she said if they said it they got it wrong. I thought it might relieve you that it wasn't the heart. I know how it is. Since I had that lump, if anyone even mentions a breast I go into a decline. Take care of yourself."

Beth was trapped in the words. Slowly a shadow possessed the garden where she sat as she read them over again. The throats of the lilies were filled with dusk. The lavender spikes had lost their sheen. And slowly the shadow possessed her body. She seemed to have taken the boat to the island and could not get off when the others did. She sank to the deck. She could hear the lapping of waves on the prow. She could feel the rocking of the cradle boat. Mysteriously she had just been born. The voices of those on the wharf died away. In the silence she heard the beat of her heart faintly, faintly till it died away.

With an effort she stood and walked in the garden. The familiar numbness dawned in her limbs. And deep in her breast her weary heart was the seagull falling into the sea.

And Camelot? Had it been nothing more than the light on the sea? She had glanced away to dip her brush into paint. She had wanted to fasten the light to paper and make it forever, and when she looked back it wasn't the same.

She sank into the old, safe pattern of her days. Painting in the mornings. The walk through the garden. A prelude on the spinet, but after a rest. Her doctor smiled to have her back on track, while he listened to her chest as if it were a shell through which he heard the sea. Her father came around to sit and stroke her hair. He was carving her some figures from the fairy tales. Eric held her lovingly and kissed her hair. And Marian dropped by to brighten an hour with her bronzed sweet flesh. When the two of them were with her she sensed the ripeness that cried for plucking. They would not taste until she left the room . . . It was easier now to look away. Perhaps again it was the light on the water and when she looked back it would be another thing.

They were all relieved and happy to have her in place. And she herself . . . she herself was relieved. It had been too hard for her in Camelot. The terrible need to make the most of it. To make the death of Peter Kilbourne count for something. To use his gift well. Now she could recall him as loving and generous but, alas, mistaken. She could mourn him as the dearest friend she would ever have. She read his gentle books over again. Her recovery was a story he'd invented for her but she had reached the end. Camelot had been a sweet and bitter place. A troubled dream. She could not have borne it another day.

She tried not to miss him on their trips to the lake. She would paint the water from their clump of birches and recall how they had met. How he had come to watch her and tell her she was good, very good, but there were lakes in the hills . . . She cried a little. No one in her life had ever loved her so much.

Three years had passed since the word of his death. They were at the lake again, and someone was in the cottage he had rented before. A man younger than Peter but older than herself. She had seen him from afar. She was painting the water, and he walked through the birches and stood at a distance looking at her. When she felt his eyes upon her she turned and smiled faintly.

He waited a little and then he came to her. "You are Beth," he said in a resonant voice.

She looked up in surprise, her brush poised for a stroke. He had a long El Greco face. A small pointed beard. "I knew Peter," he said. "I knew him quite well. He told me of you."

Her dark eyes misted. "You knew him?" she said.

"Quite well. We were the best of friends. After he was too ill to stay here for long I would take the cottage for the rest of the summer. He hated to release it."

"I miss him so much. Are you a writer too?"

"No, I'm a painter. I see we have that in common. Besides Peter," he said.

"And he told you about me?"

"Yes, he did. Quite a lot . . . Are you quite well now?"

She looked at him in amazement.

"Forgive me," he said, "but he told me about it. He had a great faith in what he was doing. A tremendous faith. He made a convert of me." He smiled at her. "In a crisis in my own life he accomplished it wonderfully, but it was nothing so great as what he undertook in yours."

She searched his face.

"May I?" he said. "You're dripping water on your paper." And he took away her brush and put it in the glass.

"How did he die?" she asked softly.

"It seemed to be painless, I'm happy to tell you. I was with him at the time. We were speaking of you. And then he grew too exhausted to speak. We sat quietly together. And suddenly he put his hand to his chest and he was gone."

"It was his heart?"

"It was his heart. And so you see . . . It was wonderful. I was so glad to be there. Otherwise I might have begun to doubt that he had done it. It's really an extraordinary thing, as you know . . . I heard from the caretaker that you came here alone, that you seemed to be thriving."

She could not speak. Her trembling hand had tipped the glass.

His voice was kind. "What is it?" he said.

To be given the burden of life again. I cannot bear it, she wanted to cry.

White Hyacinths

On Wednesday nights in the fall and winter and in the spring before it got too warm, the string quartet played in the basement room of the oldest house on Tenth Street. Hobson, who was second violin, owned the house and lived there with his antique mother. In the past he had insisted that they play upstairs in a respectable parlor, but there was something about the basement room that captured the imagination. There was a certain devilish charm in making music below the ground, in sending it up to trip the feet of passers on the sidewalk and to draw them stealthily across the ragged lawn of the ancient house to spy downward through the narrow windows. The players were used to seeing several sets of mortal legs an evening. Whenever they appeared placarded against the dimly lighted night—these legs at which the players never glanced precisely—an amused self-consciousness galvanized the group below; their separate bodies swayed with perceptible rhythm, their bows arched with infinite grace, and it seemed to the four of them as if they played like angels.

Being amateurs, they had a lively need of these legs. Indeed, the legs were sometimes all they had. Except, of course, whatever it was that drew them on the cruelest nights of winter and the stormiest nights of spring. Neither snow, nor rain . . . nor gloom of night, nothing stayed them from their appointed Wednesdays. Certainly the love of music drew them. There was more . . .

Jason, who was first violin and most accomplished of the group, expressed it with a certain diffidence on one occasion. "It's an oasis," he began and stared along the length of his bow as if it were an arrow he was pointing at the great black-bellied furnace in the corner. He avoided the eyes of the other three. "We live in an unholy city full of noise and soot and the waste of spirit . . ." It was clear he had re- hearsed the words. And they did seem a little much to the rest. Were they not committed, or virtually so, to expressing the inexpressible with music? It was like betrayal to have found the words. Jason himself grew sorry to have found them. "And so it is . . ." He glanced at Maria, who played viola. More and more what he said was said for her. Her dark, responsive eyes were fixed upon his own. "And so it is," he repeated, his voice rising on a note of warmth, "we come together for one night a week to make for ourselves a little peace." He looked at them shyly and yet with a challenge. "We make it together. That's the thing."

Hobson coughed. Arthur, the cellist, brushed the strings of his in- strument with his palm. Their smiles were restrained. But the eyes of Maria in serious approval held Jason's eyes. In her olive face and slender form he had come to find all purity and wisdom. Her high cheekbones and black-as-raven eyes reminded him of legends: Indian maidens leaping over waterfalls and into canyons, and in the fullness of a moment seizing womanhood and knowledge.

She offered now, "It's making something . . . well, of beauty too."

There was a pause. "Of course," they cheered brightly to ignore the pause. They were ignoring, too, the last movement of Schubert's quar- tet. It had gone quite bad in the middle. That was why they had needed the encouragement of high purpose.

Now, all of this happened in the spring, their first together after playing through the fall and winter. Summer came and the furnace died. An odor of earth invaded their nest. In the damp they would pause to tighten their strings. The notes would blur in the marshy air. The season seemed to have moved against them when, sadly, Hobson was off to Maine. A yearly custom. The heat, he said. His mother's survival was clearly at stake. And so for the summer they gave it up.

But Jason proposed to Maria alone on the final night they played together that perhaps on the weekends the two of them might find a spot for practice. Above the basement room they lingered on the side- walk in the thickened air. They were trapped in the breath of motors and the haze beneath the streetlight. Their spirits, which had expanded, were wounded by the city. They had laid aside their armor for two hours at the least and had not slipped it on again to battle with the world. The music they had made below was haunting them still. Somewhere in the sooty branches of the trees it lingered.

She rested her dark, troubled eyes upon him. "My parents live in New Mexico. They have sent for me." With the back of her hand she wiped the moisture from her cheek. "All spring I have not gone. But now I must."

He could taste his disappointment. "Keep safe," he finally told her. And when she looked up he was moved to say, "You belong to us now. You hold our music in your hands. You have a grave responsibility."

She gave a fleeting smile. "That is too much to say."

"You must think of it all summer," he said into the shriek of tires. Asking it, he held his breath: "You will come back to us at last?"

"I have my work at the college. I type for them."

Something curiously stilted was always in her speech. At first he had thought it her native shyness. Then he came to think that all the warmth and silken ease had gone into her music. Some god had placed it there instead of in her words. At times he longed to tell her. But he grew afraid of frightening her away. Or of frightening himself. For the time he was content to speak to her in music. While the others played beside them, they withdrew. They circled one another, moving closer, light and shadow, almost touching, never quite. Sometimes in crescendo he cried out to her alone and heard her brooding answer, and they might have found each other or lost their way. But always they were saved and sheltered by the others. "Will you miss our Wednesday nights?"

"Yes. Oh, yes."

"And I shall miss you."

She frowned a little. Then she said, for a reason that was never clear to him, "My mother is Mexican." Whereupon she drew her lips together and turned away her olive cheek. She seemed to him remote and more than ever like the legend. And her silence seemed to lengthen into all his summer days. The trucks that ran at night had begun to shrill their presence a half a block away. He wanted to hold her, to shut away her ears that were made for music. "She's in your playing," he told her. "A singing . . . a rhythm."

At that she smiled so beautifully that he took heart and wrote to her two letters to be forwarded by the college. They were all about music, but they were never answered.

All the summer long he drove to the office and handled real estate insurance and moldered in the heat. But in the evenings he returned to his upstairs room and shut the door in order not to see the pained annoyance of his landlady. He opened the windows she kept closed all day and practiced trills and double stops and finally something sad and sweet, which somehow brought the autumn closer when the Wednesday nights would resume.

After two years in the city he was still a stranger. At thirty-nine he had matured into impatience with the present and the past. And things that held futility at bay were to be cherished.

It was not he but Hobson who had devised and placed the notice in the paper. "Wanted," it had said, "competent violinist, violist, cellist to play with violinist in his home. For pleasure only." For salvation, Jason felt he might have added. For the white hyacinth to feed Mohammed's soul. He had recalled the prophet's words: "If I had but two loaves of bread, I would sell one of them and buy white hyacinths to feed my soul."

Curiously, only the three of them had answered. Those three and no more . . . which gave the thing a pleasant feel of destiny. A woman might have muddied things, but happily she hadn't. Arthur, remotely English, was jovial but reserved with her. His fervors were all for the cello, it seemed. His brief moustache was beginning to gray, and his splendid aquiline nose had taken on a sharpness. At times when they were playing he seemed to doze between the movements. Besides, he had a wife, though sadly an unmusical one. And Hobson, looking with his bald pate like a genial, celibate friar, had his mother . . .

Only Jason had no one. But more and more the prophet's hyacinths took on the olive shade of Maria's cheek. More and more the music and the hyacinths were one . . . Jason found a phrase of Haydn so expressive of her that he played it all the summer with longing and delight.

But October always comes, and though the weather was still warm, the quartet met at last in the basement room. It was such a relief to play again together, so much more satisfying than anything that any of them had done all summer that Maria cried a little; to cheer her up they played a Schubert rondo. Jason dedicated it especially to her. She thanked him with such eloquent eyes that he was sure she must have gotten both his letters.

The four of them agreed the basement room was the loveliest room in all the world. What other had an aging furnace of such charm to claim its corner? Or such a sweet, untidy look, with its wormy upright piano to grace another and its litter of half a century thrust cozily into others and its assortment of fusty discarded chairs astray about the floor like pigeons feeding in the square. It was just as they had left it in the spring, for Hobson vowed he hadn't dared to clean it for fear of breaking down with sorrow at their absence.

The four of them were lovers rediscovering one another after separation, exploring delightful intimacies of musicianship in each. Maria's warm, dramatic softness was restored to them, Jason's expert trills, Hobson's sweetness, which drifted from the surface of his strings like morning mist. They were prompted to recall that Arthur, who in all else observed an Englishman's restraint, became as fiery as any Latin in his playing. Scraping his bow, he swayed and bent and dipped in quite exaggerated fashion, as if he trusted by sheer bodily excess to whip the inner man to musical response. At times he seemed to wrestle with a bear.

Everything seemed good to them. Even when Hobson brought his aging mother down to savor their formal opening, they found it in their hearts to give enthusiastic greeting, to be delighted at her state of preservation. But they did not press her to remain, remembering her visits of the winter past. There had been times when Hobson's mother, like Whistler's, had sat frail and placid in her chair. But at other times she indicated a desire to play. Then her son would lead her, tottering, to the old upright that blocked the corner, gently propping her before the keyboard. And politely they would rummage behind the furnace for a quintet, usually Schumann's in E flat. It always startled them, the vigor with which her gnarled old fingers struck the keys. She played from memory since her eyes no longer read the notes. Surprisingly, she got it back as she hummed aloud the melody up into the musty ceiling, down into her hands. But they would not believe, as Hobson vowed, that she had been a fine concert pianist in her season. Something was lacking. Her pauses, which should have soared with music unsounded, instead were like bird bodies fallen from the sky. At times there was a hint of ragtime in her Schumann. Such things are not infirmities of age.

But tonight she sat and listened absently while they played again together, while they rediscovered the familiar pieces and their graces, greeting with delighted cries the old composers they had parted from last spring, Arthur calling, "Good old Schubert! Splendid fellow! Good old Brahms!" They finished nothing. They sipped and tasted some of all—like riotous plunderers loose in a cellar of wine.

As if the parallel occurred to him, Hobson disappeared and brought down from the upstairs region a bottle of imported claret he had bought for the occasion. He served it in the silver wine cups—a gift, he told them, to his mother from an early musical admirer. And all was merrier than ever.

Tonight the passersby who heard the merry voices and the music and stepped across the ragged lawn to spy were intrigued to see below a band of four musicians and an old, old lady and a furnace almost half as old. It had sounded rather like a rathskeller newly opened by some enterprising, homesick German of the city.

It must not be supposed that they caroused. After all, one bottle of wine among the five—for the old lady let a cup of it be pressed upon her—and a portion of it dashed upon the rusty belly of the furnace in a spirit of recognition of its place in their joint lives. The wine was quickly gone. And rather than a rathskeller, the basement was transformed into a palace room where centuries ago musicians played to some exalted few. They filled it with a sweet, confined, and private sound, which had indeed an Old World charm. They fashioned a performance and at once a conversation. And Hobson's mother sat and listened, or seemed to listen, like an ancient princess who had long survived her time.

Toward the end of the evening, in the midst of a noisy tarantella, she fell asleep in her chair. The wine they had given her had tipped and stained the skirt of her gray dress and lay in a blood-red pool beside one shoe. "Poor mother," said Hobson, "she is getting old." They would not notice that her face was strange.

For tonight they felt inviolate.

But as if a clock had struck, it seemed a signal to end the evening. After the tarantella they parted, speaking in hushed tones so as not to wake the sleeper. It was by now so late that with regret they decided to forgo the customary roll and coffee at the shop just down the street.

Maria was full of dreaming when Jason drove her home. For the first time she allowed it. They rode and scarcely spoke. The music had made for them a bond and yet a barrier. Their silence was fragrant with the smell of burning leaves. Once he said, with a schoolboy's indirection, "I think you must have practiced quite a lot this summer." And in the dark she smiled and said, "No more than you."

But when he took her to the door he held her hand and told her steadily, "I have a great desire to take you home like this each Wednesday night," and when she did not draw away her hand, he ventured, "It will make a good beginning . . ."

The curve of her cheek was golden in the lamplight from the hall. All the summer was between them like tears they must shed.

With his free hand he touched her dark rain-cloud of hair. "Your Mexican mother," he said. He was recalling the only confidence between them. And she smiled. They stood for a moment thinking of her long summer days, with her mother's hair beneath his hand alive, more alive than the strings of his violin.

Then he took away his hand and let his voice grow happy.

"Sometimes when we all play steadily for several hours, like tonight, I feel so tired but so . . . at peace. I feel at home. The basement room is my home. When I leave . . . but I never leave it. I live there all the week . . . I have always lived there."

An autumn wind was rising in the trees beyond the doorstep.

"Yes," she said. And she drew away her hand, but gently. "It's getting late."

"Late?" he said into the rising wind. "It's the beginning of the world."

And that was all. He drove back across the city past the shrinking downtown lights. In the beginning there were four of them together. Making music against the world. He liked the phrase. And thinking it, he picked four distant lights like a chord of music and shaped his fingers on the steering wheel to form it. He drew his mind across it like a bow and listened in his heart to hear its fullness. And then he raised his hand and placed his fingers gently on the two lights closest . . . But he did not draw the bow. Something lyric in his nature sang itself into desire and would not be startled or hastened by the flesh.

He met the lights and passed them by. The theme would be developed. Together they would add their glorious variations, but nothing would be taken away.

Tonight there was such music in her hands, her hair, and in her every motion that he dreamt of her and held her music in his arms all night.

Nothing, after all, remains unchanged. And the best things seem to change more readily than others . . . Before the following Wednesday Hobson called them all to say that he was taking his mother to Atlanta for an operation. Not much hope at her age, but it was all that one could do. The three of them expressed their sorrow. They had a guilty memory of the tarantella they had finished while the wine was pooling at her feet. But art is self-absorbed. And they were secretly consoled by the hours they had sacrificed to Schumann's quintet. With admirable restraint no one mentioned the quartet. It was understood to be of less importance than one's mother. But one could privately mourn for the interruption . . . Not to sound lively was difficult indeed when Hobson told them each in turn of his arrangement for a substitute, a fellow he had once encountered.

A splendid musician. But a little . . . it was hard to say. He was foreign, European. Hadn't been here long, but he could play. That is, it turned out that Hobson hoped he could play. It seemed that he had never heard him after all. But then he, Hobson, was looking to rejoin them in a month or six weeks.

Now, that was rather fine of Hobson, thinking of their quartet and making arrangements, with all the other on his mind! It was indeed a thing with a life of its own, almost one of God's creatures for whom provision must be made.

They only hoped this fellow—what was his name? Rostov—could play. All Hobson seemed to know was that he owned a violin.

And so, on the following Wednesday night, with hope and curiosity and some misgiving but on the whole with hope—for music kept them young in spirit—they arrived one by one at the basement room on

Tenth. The fellow, after all, was possibly very good. Foreigners had a natural bent for music, it was said.

Jason and Arthur took off their coats. At last the nights had cooled, but the basement room perversely held some of the warmth of summer. While they waited for the newcomer, the two of them made quite a business of opening the stubborn high basement windows, which Hobson naturally had fastened when he left. Maria watched them, quietly smiling and sometimes running with a childlike solicitude to steady the chairs they stood upon. They wished to conceal the sharp expectancy they felt. But amid this flurry of opening the windows the men kept stealing glances through the muddy panes. And Maria, with her dark-as-raven eyes, grew still. She was more than ever like the Indian child-maiden who waits for her lover by the waterfall that is soon to hurl them both into an ageless wisdom.

At last the windows were open and the chairs were placed again exactly as found, for the order of disarray must never be altered. Then Arthur breathed heavily through his splendid nose and ruffled his brief moustache. "Past time. Could be he couldn't find us." He looked across the room at the instruments in their cases laid beside the high piano. "Hobson's vague on directions. Very bad. Couldn't find the place myself a year ago. A foreigner . . ." he began, but he did not finish. The furnace in the corner gave a sudden belch, the small explosive noise to which a furnace is inclined. But they did not laugh. They were suddenly anxious.

All at once they heard a step above them at the door connecting basement with the house above. To their surprise this door above the stairway was opened, and slowly a stocky figure backed into their view. One foot was carefully thrust behind it to the step below, then a shabby violin case made an awkward arc to the rear. The door was pushed but failed to close. It dragged at the bottom with a scuffling sound. The foot thrust backward was withdrawn. A shoulder was applied to the door. There ensued a general elevation of the rear of the figure. And all the while the grubby violin case, peeling a little at the edges, was dangled above the astonished faces below.

He turned and faced them uncertainly, as if fearful of falling from the ladder-like stair. They saw a flattish head with short gray untidy hair, the hairline receding from the narrow brow, heavy eyebrows, dark pendulous eyes rather like the sorrowful eyes of a hound, gray cheeks not freshly shaven, rough, shapeless mouth with a bulbousness between lip and chin. All this above a round-shouldered stocky frame, which was queerly clothed in a stained belted jacket and brown serge pants.

They stared at him in embarrassment. They felt they should smile, but happily his pendulous eyes moved past them in a slow, indifferent tour of the room.

"I say," Arthur managed, "we're jolly glad you're here. Hobson, you know . . . We had no idea you were up there all along . . ."

Rostov came carefully down the steps, his violin case thrust before him. When he stood among them they drew back from him instinctively. "Is ready," he said. The words had a soft foreign blur. Now at close range they saw the heavy, lax muscles of his face, the twofold crease between nose and mouth. And he really seemed not to have shaved for some time.

What bothered them most was his air, not of stupidity perhaps, but of vacancy. No light anywhere in face or gesture. Where was the spark to fire the hands for the strings and bow? They sighed within themselves.

They bore his indecision and watched him cross the room to the old piano where their instruments lay. He laid his own case along the keyboard, unlatching it heavily to the muffled protest of the keys beneath. Mechanically they followed. And when he drew forth a mellowed beauty of a violin, finer than anything of theirs, they smiled at one another in sheer relief. With a thing like that surely the fellow could play. Surely too it explained why Hobson had engaged him to join them and even to take up his residence here.

Politely they gave him a moment. Then they unsheathed their own instruments and reassembled in the customary pattern, moving to their places with the swift, sure grace of fencers. They enjoyed the ritual of making ready—the assembling, the tuning, the passing out of scores. They performed it neatly. Then they waited for Rostov. The fellow was awkward for a fact, flailing his arms about and dropping his score . . .

Jason had determined on an early quartet of Beethoven, one not difficult but up to the musical and technical standards of the group. He rapped on his chair. Silence. In unison they began the first movement. The bowing of the three was brave and alert; their tone was passionate yet crisp. They played for the stranger dropped into their midst. They wished him to see what must be his measure. They yearned even to stir him, to make him marvel. So at first their own music enraptured them. The Greek youth bends to his own reflection. But now they were listening for the stranger. Was he with them? His playing was muted . . . With one accord then they abated their tumult. And Jason acknowledged with a prick of chagrin their excess of bravura.

In a small crescendo there came his silken purity of tone, soaring, sustained, then winging downward to a phrase curved and warm as a feathered throat . . .

Arthur missed a bar. "I'm sorry . . ." he began. They had all stopped.

"From the beginning," Jason said and rapped. He was conscious that Maria's eyes were on him. Silence. Again. This time Maria came in two beats late. She made no apology, although the silence cried out for a word, an impatient gesture.

Jason kept his eyes on the dusty floor and on Maria's small foot as she drew it away and under her chair. Sometimes a slight thing marks a turning point. Later, he recalled a small foot being withdrawn as the turning. Slowly he lowered his violin. From the furnace came a smell of last winter's ash, faintly pungent with a summer's decay. He held his breath. "Shall we try something else?" They waited for him while he fluttered the pages. "Shall we try the Rasoumovsky? I think the first." Out of sheer perversity he chose the difficult.

Even as they lifted their bows to begin, they were conscious of legs dimly lit and framed by the windows. The players below were struck with reluctance. Jason held his bow in midair and lowered it and raised it again in the silence. Defiant of the legs, without a sign to the others he drew his bow. And only Rostov was with him, playing with such dominion and grace that Jason's playing almost failed before it. Then the other two scurried across the bars, to catch up at last like breathless children. The sad little discords that followed their flight were not even painful but brave disharmonies. They were only the cracked, broken voice of the music, a senile voice, a battered recording with the grooves worn through into other grooves. Hearing it, Jason despaired in his heart.

All evening they played deplorably. At times the music recovered its breath. But Rostov would solo for several bars. Then Arthur or Maria would be late in joining, perhaps off key. Sometimes Jason sent them back to the beginning. More often he let them stumble to a finish. Through it all the golden thread of Rostov was woven. It did not proclaim or assert itself; it was there in the sorry fabric of their evening, unmistakably lustrous and round and firm. It might have been drawn out whole and shining and the rest of the evening tossed into the furnace with the smell of the ash and mercifully burnt when the nights grew cold.

Once, in a passage for violins, he and Jason played several bars in unison; then in fugal flight each turned and twisted through the path of the other. In and out they glided, weaving, dipping, like swallows at play. Lips thinned and set, Jason knew the flash of the stranger's phrasing, knew the shimmering passage of the glistening bird, now above, now beside him, and now below . . . Once for a moment Jason lost his place. But on the whole his bird flew surely. Like a bright toy bird at the end of a stick that children whip into noisy flight.

Several times Jason glanced across at Maria. Her dark hair had fallen against her cheek. Her face was flushed and almost startled. Her eyes were luminous with joy.

Jason's throat was dry. He felt a knot at the pit of his stomach. Usually they took an intermission at nine and then resumed for another hour. But Jason drove them on till nine-thirty. Then he said, "Shall we call it a night?" It was hardly a question.

They paused, breathing heavily. All except Rostov, who sat quite still, his stocky figure bagging around his chair. Jason looked at his pale and heavy face. "Rostov, I'm afraid we've made rather a mess of your first evening with us . . ." Rostov did not protest. He did not even seem to be listening. "But you see . . ." Jason was watching Arthur ruffle and smooth his brief moustache with a nervous finger. "You see, the technical excellence has always been incidental with us. The coming together . . . the playing together has always been the great thing with us." Unconsciously his eyes sought Maria's for support. But she looked away from his into the air, as if she were ashamed of his words.

Then she raised her eyes and rested them on Rostov. "I wonder," she said quietly, "if you would play something for us before we go. Anything at all."

There was a pause. Rostov looked at them all with a questioning face. He put his hand to his mouth and coughed.

Maria said softly, "It is late, of course."

And Rostov glanced at her over his hand. "Is late," he said through his crumpled fingers. The nails were broken and grayed with soil. He nodded as if they were sharing a secret. Then he took away his hand and smiled at it with a corner of his mouth. And all at once his weariness was a palpable thing. His head was bent. His body looked suddenly chilled and cramped. He drooped in his chair like a helpless old man left huddled in the doorway with the sun gone down and no one come back to move him inside. Maria gazed at Rostov with rapt compassion, as if they two were alone in the room.

Jason rose. They all rose and began to put away their instruments. Tonight there was none of the tired exhilaration of other Wednesday nights that came from drinking together the wine of making music. There was something of the feeling that each had struggled separately and lost, that the cup had been dashed from the undeserving lips.

Slowly Jason took his tweed coat from the corner and put it on and straightened his tie. Then he turned to Rostov and watched him struggle into his own dingy garment. To be precise, it was hardly a coat. It was more like a jacket worn by a hunter, fashioned as it was of a kind of canvas, worn of elbow and spotted of collar, and on the pocket a suspicious stain as if it had once held a quarry of sorts.

"Rostov, we have a custom," he said with irony. "After these sessions we visit a coffee shop down the street. We reward ourselves for a successful evening . . . You will join us?"

There was a feeling almost alive in the room that if Rostov would refuse and go upstairs, then something of the evening might still be saved. Even in Maria Jason knew the feeling, knew almost the wish. These evenings were not to be cast away. This night was the product of one full year, but surely of more, if time be measured by the clock of the spirit.

They watched him on the brink of refusal. They sensed as well his desire to refuse. And then on an instant they knew his kind; wanting to refuse, even knowing the general will for his refusal, he could not force the words to free them all. He was like a weary guest in the doorway of his weary host, and both of them so long for his departure. And yet it seems impossible to leave. Is it weakness? Perversity? Despair? He said, "I will come," in an accent more foreign than before, and did not look at them again.

And so they all trudged up and out into the night air that had a cold, dry taste of winter. Jason's car was at the curb, but there had always been a voiceless agreement that walking was the thing. After an evening of working with the arms there was a rightness in using the legs. Now they moved off briskly, the dead leaves covering the sidewalk sounding a dry vibrato beneath their feet.

They liked going into the shop together with their instruments clutched in their hands. They made it a point to enter in order: first violin, second violin, viola, and then Arthur bringing up the rear, his cello lifted high above the floor with a certain awkward grace. People turned to stare, to surround them with an aura of strangeness. They always went past all the tables to the rear and their accustomed booth.

But tonight Rostov waited for the others to precede him. He waited for them to place their instruments carefully on the table of the booth next to theirs (Arthur propped his in the corner), to seat themselves and make room for him. Then he stood for a moment before them, looking vaguely about, and at last drawing up a chair to sit outside the booth at the end of the table. He placed his violin in its battered case across his lap, and rested upon it his shabby sleeves. He was very much in the way of the girl who came to take their order.

Jason glanced at them all and cleared his throat. "Rostov," he said, "it's always been sweet rolls and coffee. Just a custom we have." Then a faint, dry irony stirred in his voice. "Of course, if you've worked up an appetite . . ."

Rostov looked at the walls of the booth. They sensed in him an old longing. Perhaps hunger. His eyes deepened, and he stroked his violin case with the palm of one hand. "The roll," he said softly and finally.

"Coffee?" the waitress prompted.

He shook his head. After all he did not seem hungry. Only a little sick.

But they would not stare. While they waited for food they tried to recapture the easy comradeship of other Wednesday nights in the coffee shop. But tonight it would not come. Arthur was looking a little dazed. The overhead light was making brown circles beneath his colorless eyes. He was almost remote and divorced from them all. On other nights in the shop they'd felt married to Arthur, often sorry for his sadly unmusical wife. For Arthur, after wrestling with his cello all evening, would unfold and expand and bestow on his chosen the congeniality of wedlock. In his own reserved way he was comfortable and confiding. He was lovable and loving. They felt they had lived with him half their lives. More than that was the pledge that he seemed to have given them: You are my chosen, my best beloved. Indeed they were all pledged, each to the other in a sort of marriage in which there was still romance and gaiety . . . Hobson's departure had left them bereft of a lawful mate.

And now here they sat, as if this whole splendid and intricate knot could be untied in a single evening. They had not once thought to mourn for Hobson.

Maria sat too erect, her eyes on her beautiful, sensitive hands folded among the crumbs of the table. When the roll and coffee came, Jason tasted of each. He said with a certain hardness of tone, "We might try a barbershop quartet. Might be more successful."

No one thought it was funny. They might at least have smiled. He sipped his coffee, which tasted bitter. His roll was dry and stale, but he kept on eating in a mounting despair. All the while he longed to take Maria's hand. It moved him to see that she was not eating. He thought, I have got her mixed up with this music and I cannot separate one from the other. He hungered to touch her face and her hair till tears came to his eyes and he stared into his coffee. Tonight . . . tonight he would take her home and tell her all that was in his heart. Thinking of the joy of it, he raised his eyes to hers.

But she was looking at Rostov, who seemed, Jason thought, the last thing to be looked at. He appeared oddly graceless, sitting there leaning over his roll, not eating, just leaning in a vacant way. Then, as they all watched, he picked it up and began to unroll it slowly, deliberately, while bits of clear icing, an occasional raisin, tumbled untidily into his plate. It was somehow a gesture for them of defiance, almost an irreverence, when, never pausing till he reached the small curl of dough in the center, moist and dark with cinnamon, he neatly detached this final nugget, this crux, this ultimate thing redolent of sugar and spice, and popped it into his open mouth.

It became the final outrage. After that there was nothing more to be said. Arthur finished and slid his way out of the booth. Rostov, when he found himself blocking their exit, rose as well. And so with relief they all said good night. Rostov walked out through the now vacant room. Arthur followed with his cello held absurdly high.

But Maria herself made no move to go, and Jason saw it with a tremulous joy. Without looking at her he savored the fullness of their being alone. After the waitress had cleared away the mess that Rostov had made, he began to feel peace. It was even as if he had taken her home and had told of his love on the steps of her house, as if this evening had never been. He smiled at her bowed head. "He's something out of comic opera," he said.

She drew her folded hands away from the table. But she did not look up.

He waited a little. He told her, as if to explain their silence, "We speak in music. Our tongues are chained."

"Why do you bait him?" She looked up at him suddenly with strange, dark eyes.

"Bait him?"

"Yes, bait him."

"But what did I say?"

She stared at the waitress stacking plates in the corner. "It's the way you say it."

Someone laughed and called out from the kitchen beyond. He reminded himself that often she was not at ease with her words. He said quietly and sadly, "I don't think I understand your word 'bait.'"

She pushed her dark hair away from her forehead, and her eyes on the waitress were cold and unfriendly. "Why do you resent him?"

He found himself silent, alone and dismayed.

She looked back at him quickly. "Because he's foreign?"

"I don't resent him." He spoke impatiently.

She stared into the booth across the room. "I am foreign."

His mouth tightened. "You're not to me . . . I wouldn't care if he wore a ring in his nose."

She began to put her handkerchief into her purse, and when she had finished she laid her purse neatly on the table before her and folded her hands. "Because he plays so well."

He gazed at her angrily. The clock above them struck with a whirring sound.

"How can you say that?"

She rose and started out. It seemed to him there were tears in her eyes.

"Don't go now . . . please. Let me take you home."

But she shook her bent head. He did not press her. Silently he helped her with her coat. Outside, he said, "I'll see you next Wednesday." And when she nodded, not looking at him, he grasped her sleeve. "What have I done?" She looked into the night.

Two girls were passing, each laughing into the face of the other. She turned to watch them. A neon sign colored her face red, then gold . . . red, and then gold. He laughed sadly, touching her red-gold cheek. "You said such a hard thing in there just now. You should ask my forgiveness. But we'll try it another way. I'll ask yours. Forgive me, please . . . for whatever I've done."

She broke away and walked down the street. He thought of going after her, of crying, "I love you." But a bus roared past. She began to run.

He drove slowly back to the house where he lived. When he reached his room, he lay on the bed without a pillow beneath him. He lay there thinking deliberately of Rostov, not standing shabbily at the top of the stairs, nor plucking the roll with his yellow fingers . . . but of Rostov bent over the violin, playing the Beethoven, playing the Brahms . . . and then imperceptibly shifting to notes never heard before. Notes of such beauty that the air sang with them, the soul expanded. And it seemed to Jason—he was dreaming now—that his heart would break with the rapture of them.

Trembling with them, bathed in light, he raised his own violin and his bow and was only waiting for the sign to begin. His fingers pulsed with the gathering joy. In gladness he cried, "It's doing it together." But the cue never came. Suddenly behind him Maria murmured so clearly that he heard her words thrust in like a song: "He is all we need."

He awoke then, slowly, with tears in his eyes. He lay there, throat aching with the fullness of tears. A whole week of emptiness. A winter of nothing. Damn him, he whispered. He has trampled the green grass of the beautiful oasis.

Before the next Wednesday winter came to the city. The buses were topped with frost in the mornings. Breath was white in the morning and evening. Even at noon the wind blew cold. Less than ever was one man enough for himself.

They were all relieved that the basement room was as warm as recalled from the winter before. Hobson had arranged a fire in the furnace. It might have been more bohemian to have played with their fingers cold perhaps. The thought occurred, but they needed warmth to surround their spirits still chilly from the week before. The three arrived not three minutes apart. Puffing and blowing on their frozen hands and rushing ahead to rub their cold backs on the great old giant, who dozed in the corner, and throwing their arms about his dirty chest, they whipped up quite a flurry of merriment. Maria with red cheeks smiled at Jason, though she never once looked into his eyes.

They were warming their backs against the furnace, lined up half-circling it, side by side like three cheerful martyrs at a common stake, when Rostov arrived. He backed in as before to retreat down the steps and up them again to lift the door into place, while he dangled behind him above their heads his scrubby case, like an unsavory fish he was offering to sell. And when he faced them he looked so exactly the same as before that they could but stare. Same jacket, same expression. No glint of recognition in his pendulous eyes that he had ever seen them before.

"Greetings!" Arthur called.

Rostov descended the steps with care.

"It's cold out," Maria announced.

His eyes swept the room. "Is cold. Yes." He accepted the cold. Perhaps he had stayed in the house all week, for his skin was touched with a deeper pallor. His sad, drooping eyes held the moisture of men who are broken with years. And all his clothes, from his sordid jacket to his brown serge pants, hung so limp, so shapeless and shiny and burnished with soil, that he might have been recently pulled from the river and never allowed completely to dry. They no more believed that this sodden creature could play like an angel than they had believed it the week before.

They resumed the business of making ready with almost the relish of other Wednesdays. But when they began the somber Schubert, the movement in C minor they had always loved, their hands were burdened with tension and fear. Gone from the face was the half-smile of pleasure and the joyous alertness. Arthur had quenched the fire in his bow. They listened as in a guilty dream to the weightless playing, the liquid phrase.

Grieg's quartet. They played it twice as a courtesy to Hobson. He had left it, a gift, on their music stands with "Bon voyage" lettered in red at the top.

Quartet in D major. Mendelssohn.

Finally, from the B flat quartet of Beethoven, the Cavatina, which the master himself had fashioned with tears. Halfway through, Maria stopped. Viola still cradled against her face, she laid her bow slowly across her lap. Her eyes on Rostov held a strange dark light, as if at last she plunged toward the truth on the floor of the canyon. Seeing her, Jason laid down his bow. His mouth was set. A page later, Arthur also stopped.

Only Rostov went on to the end. His eyes were closed. He scarcely moved. In the wake of his bow the air was charged with tenderness that kindled dreams . . .

When it was over no one spoke. Jason broke the silence with "Intermission." Maria rose and put on her coat and went up and out into the winter air. Jason found her looking up at the stars. She did not turn at his approach.

"Maria, what is it?"

She spoke in sorrow as if to herself. "Don't you see, our music is in our heads. We're so self-conscious. We set it apart. We make a cult of it. We build an altar . . ."

Her words amazed him, their ease and passion.

"But with him, it's there. It's air and food. There's never a time when it isn't there."

"Maria, what would you have me do?" Then, as she made no move to answer, "What is it you would have all of us do?"

She turned on him. "What is there to do except to listen and be thankful?"

He said it sadly, "All I know is that you no longer care if we play together. Can he change all that?"

The wind began to blow up the street. The trees bent with a shuffle of leaves. He could hear the sound of a cardboard box being whipped in darkness along the gutter.

He felt they were caught in the spell of winter. In its gathering gloom he found the words. "Once a week is never enough. We never talk. We need to talk . . . We never touch."

She seemed to hear only his naming of need. "He needs to be cared for." The sounds of the night were drowning her voice. "He needs proper food. He needs clothes . . . He needs care."

He listened with wonder and distaste to her words. "You would care for him?" he asked.

He heard her scorn. "I would do it, yes."

He spoke with caution. "I don't deny that his music is fine." What he said to her now must be said well or between them all could be lost forever. He turned from her face and tried to think only of making the words. "There is a perfection . . ."

"It's better than perfect. There's something there that tries to be perfect. You feel what he does is too good to be better, and all the time it will get to be better. It's reaching up . . . it's getting better with every note till he gets to the end, and the end is the best. And even then it goes on and on and into the way you breathe and walk."

Her eloquence stunned him. With an effort he smiled. "I love you because you're a poet," he said. He tried to ignore her indignant eyes and was sick at heart that his first word of love had been spoken with irony. "As for me, I can't separate one thing, even a fine thing, from other things. Everything is part of everything else. I see a man's music as part of himself. The man is a part of other men. The music he makes is part of their music."

Her eyes flashed. "*Our* music is part of other music. Yours and mine are a part of it. We will always have to make music together. It's all we can do, and even then . . . But not his music. It stands alone. It doesn't need anything else, to be."

She began to sound like herself in his dream. Anger came as a great relief. "Maybe it needs one other thing. Maybe the understanding heart. You, Maria, to understand."

Scorn gave her a beauty that took his breath. She countered fiercely: "What's wrong with you is that you're afraid of something better. It's worse . . it's worse than being jealous." Her voice was breaking. "There are people all over the world like that. They want everything to be mediocre. They hate it when something is more than that." She turned and thrust her words into the dark. "People like that, they make me sick, and they make the world sick. They make it sick."

In his pain he cried, "What makes me sick is lovely young ladies trying to be profound." But even as he said it he caught at her hand and tried to stay her angry flight. He entreated her, "What we had, the four of us, wasn't it good?" He was struck with despair that even now it was past for them.

But she broke away and was walking swiftly down the street, under the lights and through the wind that shifted the murky pattern of trees, moving through pools of shadow and light. He followed her, calling into the winter, "You are more to me . . . you are more than music . . ." Then she turned the corner.

Inside, the others were waiting to play. Arthur was yanking threads from his bow. The smoke of his pipe had risen in the warmth and framed the door with a rank-smelling haze. Jason walked through it and down the steps. He tried to make his voice matter-of-fact. "I'm afraid it's up. She took the bus home. She was feeling sick." He was shaken to find he had used her own word.

"So?" Arthur said. He had a maddening inflection. "Bloody sick, I'd say, to leave her viola."

Rostov appeared unaware, indifferent. Slowly he flipped the pages of a score.

Arthur studied his bow. "We could try the Beethoven trio," he said, "the one you came up with when I was sick. It's in the corner behind the furnace."

"Without viola?"

"Well, you know, I could . . ."

Jason broke in. "Let's not," he said.

But Arthur wrinkled his heavy brows. "Sometimes I'm inclined to favor a trio. It's nice and clear. I like the one in E flat, you know.

Sometimes I think the fourth instrument muddies things a bit."

Silence fell. What Arthur had said partook of heresy. Two weeks ago it could not have been spoken. Coming now, it signaled disintegration. It was like finding a bloody feather: farther on would lie the ruined bird.

Arthur probed. "Is she sick enough to stay home next week? That kind of sick?"

"How should I know?" Jason too felt sick. His palms burned. His eyes ached. He thought, I'm no boy of twenty that the light should go out. It sickened him that he did not care if he never came to this place again. He looked at Arthur's meaningless face and he did not care if after tonight he never saw it, or if never again the voice of the cello answered the cry of his violin.

They did not notice that Rostov had risen, that he swayed a little against his chair. "I tell you this. It is I it is will not come next week."

They stared at him. Jason tested himself for the start of pleasure he must surely feel.

"But we thought . . ." Arthur said in a plaintive voice, "we understood you were staying on till Hobson got back."

Rostov spread one hand and his mouth smiled faintly. "Who knows?" he said. He paused and looked around and added, "In this life." He gave it an accent stranger than ever, as if for the first time he made such a phrase in this language of theirs. But the thought seemed one he was comfortable with.

Then, while uneasily they stood and watched, slowly he put away his violin, shrugged himself limply into his jacket, and walked at last to the basement stairs.

"I say," said Arthur, to counter the awkwardness of the moment, "you did a bully thing helping us out."

Rostov paused and eyed his foot on the step. He shifted his case from one hand to the other. He groped for words. "For me, it is the same, I play." Then he nodded at having made a good answer. He walked up into the house above, leaving behind the door ajar as if it was no longer worth the struggle.

"Can you beat that!" Arthur exploded. "Just like that he won't be here next week. Just like that!" His voice grew fretful. "He probably never intended to stay."

There was silence above them. Only the old furnace caught at something like a dog with a bone, and tossed it and growled. But in a moment it settled and slept. Arthur was stashing away his cello and with finality snapping the case. His eyes were irritable under his brows. "You locking up tonight?"

"I can."

"Hobson left you a key, I suppose. It would suit me not to have a key just now . . . with open house upstairs, you know." He crossed the room and shuffled into his muffler and coat. "If the old lady misses the silver, you know . . ." He laughed at his words in a quizzical way. He mounted the steps and thumped his case. "Hobson ought to have checked him out. Getting somebody in off the street, you never know how damn good he is. Too good is no good, that's a fact, you know."

Jason did not answer. With mute indifference he watched him leave. He felt he had never liked the cello. Perhaps Casals, if one could have heard him.

The sound of the wind outside had risen. Jason got his coat and put it on. He laid away his violin. He found himself looking around the room to fix it in his memory, a room where he had been happy once. But in his weariness it blurred, and all he could see was a single chair where lay a viola lustrous and tawny, the color of honey wild and sweet as a warm string tone, the color of love. He could not move for his bitter sadness. He was thinking that people like themselves could never live simple lives of the heart. For their dreams were tangled with bloodless things, with convictions cold as a winter day, with the way a musical phrase is played. And when their hands sought one another, they must grasp these things before they touched. Before they kissed, their lips must agree. Agree as to Rostov . . . It seemed to him hard.

Wearily he walked to the furnace and pressed his back to its fading warmth. Across the room at the top of the stairs the door was ajar as Rostov had left it. Almost without a conscious decision he tucked his violin under his arm and climbed the steps into Hobson's house. It struck him with a mild surprise that never before had he entered it.

He found himself in a darkened passage. The air was cold, for the furnace below was almost out. "Rostov, are you there?" he called into space. By the light from the basement he groped his way till he found the bulb that hung from the ceiling. It clicked but with no illumination. Farther on, he seemed to see a door.

When he reached it he paused with his hand on the knob. He knocked and called. Then he opened it on further darkness. It struck him as he waited blindly that he stood in the nerve center of the house. Small currents of air were sweeping past. The stillness came from around and above. He could smell the dust.

"Rostov, are you there?" he called again. The invisible walls returned an echo. He groped in his pocket for matches and struck one. He was standing before a room that appeared to be a parlor, the respectable parlor that Hobson had offered but instinct had told them would never do. True, they had never actually seen it, but subtle havoc lies in the scene. A cornice of gilt can deflect the soaring flight of the song. A mold in the carpet imprisons its soul.

His match went out and he struck another. He found the switch by the door and pressed it. No light came on. He stood uncertainly in the doorway, holding aloft his match like a torch, thinking that Rostov had left the house.

Abruptly above him a door closed softly. He listened intently. Into the silence he shouted, "Rostov!" with a force that blew away his flame. He was suddenly angry to be trapped in darkness. As the silence endured he grew angrier still. He turned from the room, struck another match, and saw the curve of the stair beyond.

As he climbed, his match went out again, and his violin case struck against the rail. The resonance of its muffled protest sent an echo along his nerves. He struck his match. And when he found himself on a landing, his frail light quivering on a door, he shouted, "Rostov!" once again. He stepped to the door and opened it; even as his fingers groped for the switch, he knew that he would find no light.

Then he heard a sound somewhere in the house. At once a draught blew out his match. He felt the chill.

He discovered that only one match was left. A grim sort of cunning possessed him now, and he stepped back carefully against the rail. Often when he tried without his notes to play some half-remembered thing he would give his fingers to the feel of it. In return the pattern was given to him. With an effort now he freed himself from all but the steady current of air. Presently it was clear to him that the wind was rushing up the stairwell. A window on a floor above had been opened.

He did not stop to ask himself why he followed the curve of the rail. The thrill of the chase arose in him. The taste of it was in his mouth. A deep, unthinking, primal need to trap whatever lay in wait above. The bitterness of the hour past fell away down the well of the stair. And the current of air, now bracing and cold, bore him upward and toward his quarry.

When he reached the top he was scarcely breathing. The dark was complete. His fingers closed on the match in his pocket. He braced himself in the path of the current and then he stole toward the open door. He felt his way past the opening, and slowly along the wall he moved. His coat was catching in splinters of wood. Outside, the sucking of wind in the eaves was a breath in the chamber of a great bass viol.

He was moving softly along the wall until he was outside the path of the current. Then with infinite care he lowered the violin case to the floor. He straightened and drew the match from his pocket. As it blazed he sheltered it with his hand . . .

In the yellow flare his eyes took in the small room swiftly. By the open window Rostov was flattened against the wall. The shape of his body was strange, grotesque. In his face was a living terror.

Jason stared. His intoxication had grown with the hunt, but the sight of that terror was an instant check. He had thought to find Rostov at the end of the chase, but not to encounter his shrinking panic. The flame in his fingers lengthened and died. Into the darkness and the sound of the wind he called to him, "You know me, Rostov?"

The other gave a half-articulate cry.

Jason ordered, his voice rising, "Put the window down." Waiting a moment for the other to act, he then plunged toward the open window. As he struggled with the sash and bore it down, the cold air whipped and stung his face. He was amazed to see not far away the light of a lamp in a window below. The lamp belonged to another world.

In the sudden quiet he heard the heavy breath of the other. "Rostov . . . will you turn on the light." He waited. "Or tell me where." The room was still except for the sound of Rostov's breath. "Rostov, will you give us a light . . ."

Then beside him Rostov moved. He heard the whisper of his clothing. He felt an object thrust against him. It proved to be a small wax candle; then matches were passed from a trembling hand.

With the light, great shadows sprang to the ceiling and darted along the bare board walls. Nearby stood a chipped enameled table. Dripping wax against its surface, Jason stuck the candle fast. He turned to Rostov, who still was flattened against the wall. Again Jason noted the strange grotesqueness: the bloated paunch, the swollen chest. They stared in silence at one another. Slowly, holding his back to the wall, Rostov began to unbutton his jacket. He drew from his breast the violin. Then, as if it were all that had held him upright, he slid down the wall and to the floor. He sat as shapeless as a handful of clay tossed aside by the potter.

"I'm sorry, Rostov. I kept calling you."

He rubbed his face with a trembling hand. "I not know . . ." But what it was that he had not known seemed now to recede like a wave drawn back into turbulent seas. His hand drew down his eyelids gently, closing them over the pendulous eyes. Jason waited, staring down at the waxen face with the heavy wrinkles from nose to mouth. "Once in my country they come for me. Up all the steps they call my name." His voice shook. "They make the rooms to shine with lights . . . I fix it in this house no lights."

The candle glimmering on the table gave off an odor of impure wax. The pane of the window mirrored the flame. "You opened the window," Jason said.

The body swayed. "I jump . . . I cannot."

Jason turned again to the window. Below was the lamp from another world. Once, in a dream, he had sat with Maria and watched the lamplight on her hair. He had dreamt it in another world. He longed to call his senseless pursuit of Rostov a dream. He was conscious only of a void in the man, who sat on the floor with limbs unstrung, dusty, hollow as an empty wine keg. Even his breath in the air between them had the sour acridness of wine-soaked wood. It was all an illusion, Jason was thinking. We have been deceived. There was no perfection, only a kind of mechanical skill. Only facility, a trick. It is gained with practice. He felt a relief to have unmasked it, but in the act a small despair.

Rostov asked suddenly, "Why you come?"

"I needed to talk." But he did not talk. He turned from the window, and his eyes took in the room around him. An opened can upon the table. A newspaper littered with scraps of food. A dirty glass. Across a chair a ragged quilt. A dingy hat upon the floor. In the corner a heap of empty cans. All the stuff of disordered living. In the basement room three floors below the clutter was of another sort, deliberately apart from life. Here was the silt of animal existence and all its rank, insistent smell. "Did Hobson put you here?" he asked.

"Below, he tell me. Here is better." What he seemed to mean was safer.

"What are you afraid of, Rostov?"

But the fear had somehow disappeared. The muscles of his face had settled. His eyes relaxed with a dreamy look. A bald spot at the crown of his head gleamed a festive gold in the candlelight. He looked quite old but unafraid.

There was an airless chill in the room and a smell of the food scraps, a smell of wax. Jason was suddenly deathly tired. His limbs ached, and he longed with all his soul to leave. He thought of the warmth of the basement room and Maria's viola on the chair. He thought of how he would drive with it through lighted streets and knock and she would thank him . . . surely.

At last he found the words to say: "Maria left because of you. She feels I have been . . ." Wearily he searched for the word. When he had found it he could go. "She feels I have been . . . 'unthankful,' I believe she said." He waited gravely. " 'Listen and be thankful,' she said." Rostov seemed not to attend to his words, but Jason longed to have done with them. "You see, she is keenly aware of your skill . . . as are we all. If I in particular have seemed not to show it, I would have you know I am sorry for it."

A mouse was rustling among the cans. "I am in love with her," Jason said and was silent, as if he had told it all.

Now I can go, he promised himself. But he did not go. He was looking across at his violin where he had laid it on the floor and listening to the chink of the cans. Below him Rostov seemed to be dozing. Once his head gave a little jerk down and up . . . It had been a trick, like juggling. If a man does nothing all day long but practice his bowing and fingering. If he is willing to come to this . . . Jason said, "It's warm in the basement room. Be good to yourself and sleep there tonight."

Still Rostov gave no sign of hearing. Jason stooped to touch him on the shoulder. On the floor between them lay two smallish squares of paper. He could not have said where he'd seen their like, but he knew at once they were pawnshop tickets. They must have fallen from Rostov's pocket while he rummaged for candles in the dark.

Jason studied them with scorn. So Hobson was coming home at last. Somehow Rostov had divined the fact and now must leave—had he not told them so tonight?—because of these paper scraps on the floor and the sorry tale that each could tell. Poor old Hobson! Hospitable host. No more the wine from the silver cups. Nor the cup of cheer from the silver urn . . .

He asked aloud in a hard, bright voice, "Have you heard from Hobson?" and laid the tickets in Rostov's hand. He watched the yellow fingers close and slowly restore them to the jacket. And Jason thought, He's not afraid of what I will do. Only the step on the stair can move him.

Surely now he was free to go. For the fingers that played the Cavatina had stolen the cups with which the four three weeks ago had pledged themselves to music and to fellowship. The hands that took away those cups could never with tenderness crown their dreams, as if the dreams were Beethoven's own and the tears unshed were his.

Jason had traveled far this night and come to the end of it at last. He could scarcely endure his weariness. His legs were badly cramped from bending, and now he sat against the wall and stretched them out as Rostov did. He closed his eyes. The candle smoke was in his throat. The mouse was chiming the cans in the corner with all the rhythm of a little clock . . .

When he opened his eyes, across their legs was the ragged quilt he had seen on the chair. It seemed to him so strange a thing that his mind could not encompass it. He stared at the quilt in a troubled way, but it warmed his legs and he drew it closely over his lap. The mouse in the corner had gone away. The candle on the table began to gutter. But it steadied itself, and after all it would not go out. Jason drew the quilt against his chest to rest in the warmth they had trapped in it.

He seemed to be out of time in this room. He lay in his childhood cradled in warmth, and then he awoke to the pear tree in bloom. But his mother was laughing, How can it bloom? This is winter, she said. It snowed in the night . . . But the tree looks warm . . . It is, she said. It's covered with snow. And she covered him with the quilt she had made, while he stared at the warm tree, seeing it bloom, till he was the tree looking in at himself . . . Even now he was filled with the sweetness of it. The music was years away from then, but it seemed to him now he'd begun to play to bind the pear tree to himself . . .

He must have dozed. For he woke with the cry: I stare it down to make it bloom. It's only the snow I bind to myself. And all the tears he had never shed were in that cry. Maria most of all was there . . .

"Rostov," he said, "do you have a girl?"

Rostov smiled and shook his head. Then from under the quilt on the other side he drew his violin in its case. He stroked it twice. "She is my girl. She take you. You no good for more."

"Is she enough . . . Is she all you need?"

He seemed to explore the words in a whisper. "She is what is here." He was silent for a time with a brooding sternness, and his yellow fingers encircled the case as if he were back in the coffee shop unwinding his roll to the final nugget of sweetness and spice. At last he took out his violin and held it lovingly upon his knees. His yellow fingers caressed the strings till they seemed to sigh in the tops of trees.

Jason held his breath. The sigh of the strings became his breath. He knew he had dreaded this moment forever. And longed for it forever, too.

To delay it he touched the violin. "How did you get this?"

"Long ago. It was given."

Then abruptly, in a sibilant echo, up and down Rostov drew the bow: long ago . . . it was given. After that he was still, but he held the instrument against his face, now free of care and fresh as youth, with a smile as if he were listening.

He began to play softly a larghetto from Handel that sang with notes that were made of morning. It was sun on the water, cradled in water. But it changed and drew Jason down into darkness, into the whirlpool and past the drowned faces of those he had loved, soaring downward till the breath was near failing and the stifled cry could no longer be held. It seemed to him that he fell forever with the swelling cry withheld in his throat, while the bow beside him advancing, receding, and glinting with candlelight beckoned him on, till at last in the instant flare of the candle it shattered into myriad fragments of light. The light was a prism that drew him up into their midst toward the surface, away from the things he had lost and regretted, drew him away from aloneness and longing and into the red-gold heart of the prism until he was light . . . he was light itself . . . In a moment no more than a lifetime away the blue smiling face of the deep would appear and the question that lives in the soul would be answered.

All of this he had heard before when Rostov had played for him in his dream. The cry that had been in his throat was still there. And he wanted at last to say to Rostov that his bow had pierced the hard, bright shell. Hard and bright is the shell of the world. Forgive me. He wanted to seize the words: It is hard to accept the vision with grace . . .

Then the great wings folded slowly about him, softer than sleep, softer than any peace he had known.

Rostov put away his bow. "Too much is not good."

And Jason nodded. He smiled and slept.

When he opened his eyes the sun was shafting across the quilt. He was sitting up. His neck felt stiff. He studied the faded pattern of rings that lay with the sun across his knees. It gave him pleasure to look at the quilt. It was like the one that his mother had made. Each ring was part of a larger one and this, in turn, of a larger still. Like all the music he had ever loved, it was one great circle turning back into shrinking rounds and into the heart of all of them.

Even as he held it with his eyes, awareness grew that he was alone. Beyond him would be his violin where he had placed it near the door. He raised his eyes and it was gone.

In the first pawnshop he came to he saw his violin case hanging on the wall. Hanging by the handle at a gracious sort of angle, with the little white-inked cross he had long ago put just beside the handle.

For a time he stood outside the window gazing at it across the welter of homeless things, the rings and watches unreclaimed. At last he went inside the shop. The Italian woman behind the counter gazed at his unshaven face. He shut the door. In the stir of air a Chinese ornament above her head tinkled its rosy panels of glass.

"Yes?" she said. She rearranged the red fringed scarf across her breast. Her hands were plump.

And after all he could not tell her. He pointed to the violin. "Is it for sale?"

"That?" she said, and getting up she raised one fleshy arm and drew the violin off the hook. The scarf fell away but she caught it to her. Holding the case beneath her armpit, she tied the ends in a scarlet knot and smoothed it gently across her chest. She laid the case upon the counter. "Not yet for sale. It just come in."

"When will it be for sale?"

"In sixty days. It just come in." After a moment she opened the case. "You like it?" she asked.

He nodded.

She smiled at him shrewdly. "He will not be back, this man who bring it. I can tell." She laughed aloud in a happy way, and the glass panels over her head struck lightly. "For ten year now I look at them. I see which one comes back or never comes. It is in the eyes . . ." She touched her own and narrowed them gaily, "You come back in sixty days. I make you good price. Big bargain."

They stood there gazing at the violin.

"You play?" she asked.

Again he nodded.

With a graceful gesture she drew the violin from the case and swept it under her rounded chin. She lifted the bow high into the air and smiled across the polished wood, with the red scarf mirrored deep like a flame. "I tell you when I was a girl I play. In the cafe in Italy. I play for lovers." She laughed and drew the bow up and back. The heavy discord broke into her laugh. "Wonderful tone."

From somewhere in the rear of the shop a man appeared at the end of the counter. She put the violin back in its case. "You have a girl? She like music? In sixty days you play for her and it will melt her heart."

Then she went to her chair behind the counter. And the man came near and latched the case and hung it back upon the hook.

Jason went out and down the street. Into his face a winter wind was blowing the dry gray slough of the city.

He found his car and unlocked it slowly. Her viola lay in a pool of sunlight. He sat beside it. He opened the case and dropped his hand to its tawny lustre and felt how the body was warm and alive. Wild and dark and the color of honey. He was careful not to touch the strings.

Sixty days is two months . . . eight weeks. A thousand hours and half as much again . . . but not forever. It is good for a man to see the end of his penance, to know how long he must withhold his hand from what he loves. It is merciful to set the time, the day . . .

The Cloven Tree

She was slipping her fingers along the keys, flexing them lightly at the end of each run.

"Please listen to me," he was saying to her.

"I *am* listening," Abby said.

"Why can't you stop?"

"I'm practicing. You've come at a terrible time, Max dear. I have to practice every day." She was doing trills. She found she could still accomplish them, but not with the ease that she would like. "When you've reached the age of seventy-one and you've scarcely played for fifty years, you have to work at it every day." But then, as he did not offer to leave or let her be, she lifted her hands and patted his arm and turned to him with a smile and a sigh.

He sat on the bench with her, solid and square. Even his glasses were heavily chocolate-rimmed and square, too small for his ample, florid face, like dollhouse windows she would find herself looking through for Max. He was never there. If only the windows were large enough, she might have seen on the opposite wall the code of laws Max had posted for her. She had given up thinking to catch him home. He had secrets he didn't want her to share. Or else he had none and kept her at bay lest she find him dull. Max, as the world would have it, was dull. But he was her son. Their embers glowed whenever they met, and she warmed herself at the little blaze.

"I've brought you a tree," he said to her.

"A tree?"

"It's Christmas, Mama. That time again."

"It isn't yet, but that's nice of you."

"I want you to come and have a look. I have one like it for Daddy too."

"Not now, Max, dear. I'm practicing." She glanced at his face. "Later, dear."

She knew from his tone there was something unpleasant he wished her to see, so she wasn't in such a hurry about it. But after he gave up and went away, she wandered into the living room and saw it in front of the fireplace. She supposed it was meant to shock her into mending her ways. It merely struck her as quite bizarre. He had split a pine tree down the center and given her half, embellished with tinsel and colored balls. The raw, severed edge was displayed to the room, displayed to her. The spangled tree appeared struck and sundered by lightning. For this particular ruinous bolt she felt herself most surely condemned by the never visible code of laws that Max had posted for her within. His heart might have stirred with clemency, but codes for a parent know little of grace. Her eyes sought the very tip of the tree and, sure enough, the dove of peace had one leg and a wing, like something waiting its turn to be grilled. Poor Max, she thought. Why can't he get married, have a life of his own and a wife who would keep him from such excesses?

She would leave the tree standing just as it was so he couldn't rejoice that she minded it there. Max was all of fifty-two and had long since left the family nest. He managed a furniture store with ease. Without him the Chamber of Commerce would fold. And yet he behaved like an eight-year-old because his father had moved away and was living now at the end of the block.

She left the room, went into the kitchen, made some tea, and sat at the kitchen table to drink it. Through the flowered curtains above the sink she could see the oak tree shedding its leaves, and she whispered a line—from a poem, was it? "Now is the winter of our discontent . . ." Dave would know who had said it, of course. He remembered poems.

One day in the early afternoon he had come to her as she sat with her music. She had felt him behind her before she turned. "I've been thinking," he said. "If it's right for you, there's the Widow Wilson's hut in back where I can be out of your way with my stuff. It's getting a little crowded here. And I have to say the music gets in the way of things."

A pause fell like a single note. "I can always stop."

"You mustn't think of it," he said at once. His voice was warm. "I can spread out there. If it's all right."

"Of course," she said, "if it's all right with her. I thought she rents it."

"I'm paying her rent."

She had felt a little shock at that, to hear that arrangements were already made. Silently she stroked the keys. "Does this have to do with the bottle I broke?"

"Of course it doesn't. How could you ask?"

She heard him moving his boxes out. He was making several trips of it. His maps were coming down from the walls. She could hear them slither across the floor. She did not want to watch him go. She sat with her music and softly played. Finally he stood behind her again. She had always known when he was near. As if it had been in motion before, the air around her would settle a bit and then grow dense, as it does before one feels a touch. "I want you to know you can call anytime you feel uneasy. Call me anytime, day or night."

The final word struck into her heart. She had thought they were talking about the days!

"And anything else that comes up," he said. "Anything at all . . . I've given them all my billing address." She felt he had rehearsed the tone to take the chill from the words for her.

She found that her fingers were rooted in keys. Their roots grew down and into the earth. She could not turn to say goodbye.

When he was gone and the house was still she went in and lay across the bed. It belonged to her now, the whole of it . . . She lay there trying to make sense of it.

They had a room at the back of the house where he used to make all those useful things—tables, benches, toys for the children when they were young. One end of it had held his desk and all the accounting machines for his work. When he had retired he sold the machines, but the tools for working with wood remained. One day beside the planes and saws there began to appear the models of boats and shelves with books about sailing the seas. And maps on the walls of places that seemed to be far away. "What is this?" she asked.

"It's the road not taken."

"That's a poem," she said.

Then on the desk there appeared a bottle with a boat inside. "Did you make that yourself?"

"I bought it," he said.

She would pass the door and see him gazing at the ship inside. It was full of sails. Like flowers, she thought. Sometimes when she had looked in on him he seemed to be inside the bottle. Inside the ship inside the glass. She wanted to shatter the glass to free him. To free herself from having to watch him looking in.

One day she was cleaning the room for him. It had to be done when he was away. She had dusted the bottle and picked it up. She was putting it back when the boat within seemed to surge ahead. The bottle leapt from her hand and crashed. As she recalled, there had been an instant, which memory stretched to infinity, when she might, just might, have caught it up before it struck and splintered its hull on the rock of the desk and lay in the shards of its crystal shell. She was perfectly sure it had slipped from her of its own free will, but might she have saved it even so? She would never be sure, she told herself. And Dave had looked at the ruins in silence. She had placed the remains in a box for him. "I'm sorry," she said to him over and over. "I'll get you another one. Tell me where."

"Forget it," he said. "I don't need another."

She had gone to the kitchen then to think, and it came to her that she understood: Their families had summered for years at the lake. And she and Dave . . . how young they had been! There were sunlit days that flickered still in her mind like flame, and evenings sweet with heron voices that skimmed the water to haunt the wood. And her mother making her music for them, the children she loved, or for the lake. Lady of the Lake her mother was called. Their life was a story she wove for them out of the music she made at dusk. And the end was that they would fall in love. Like fish they seemed to dart below and lurk in shadows and flash in sun, and the story sank to their young ears muffled with rippling water and cries of birds. And Abby knew they would rise one day when the story was done and claim its end . . .

Yet first Dave had loved the water and boats. He told her he wanted a life at sea, but when you are young you want everything. He had a sea dream in his eyes that were bluer than any part of the lake, and he talked of boats till her mind was numb, while her fingers pressed the long dark braid that had drunk the lake and then unwove it to dry in the sun. He was planning a trip with his friend to an island. Next, they would sail down the coast of Brazil and down, down. They would round the Cape, to be gone a year. He made it so real she could see in her mind the roll of the waves and hear them break on the lonely shore. She could feel the spray. She could hear the gulls.

And then one day they had walked in the wood. She remembered it well and how he had kicked the trunk of a birch when he said to her with tears in his eyes, "You got yourself in the way of my life. I want to go on this boat trip, see, then around the world. Around the world." He was raising his voice. "I told you I wanted it all my life. You knew I did. You know the mess you make of my life."

"Go! Go!" She began to cry. "I want you to go. Who's stopping you?"

"You're so little. You're nothing at all. I could break you in two with one hand," he said. "I always hated girls who cry. So why can't I go? You tell me that!"

She started to run but he caught and held her. She struggled with him. "You think I want you to stay?" she sobbed. "You're crazy to think that. Crazy," she said. And through her tears she could see the lake. The clouds and birches were drowned in it. Her mother's music was drowned in it.

"I can tell all the time what you want me to do. I can wake up at night and know how you want me to stay here with you. I can tell it now."

He would not free her. She twisted to face him. "You want me to tell you what I can tell? I can tell it's you wanting to stay with me and wanting to hold me to blame for that."

He was crying too.

". . . Just hold you," he said.

And they cried together and then got married, and never mentioned the sea again. Even now it was never mentioned with them, but the maps had appeared and the shelves of sailing books had grown, and he had stared into the bottled ship. She knew without his having to say that now, at the age of seventy and four months and seven days, he dreamt of sailing around the world.

So that's how it is, she had thought to herself. You push things down and after a lifetime out they come. You give things up but you want them still. She had sat and looked out and into the thinning winter light and into the trees that were shedding leaves as they were today. She had felt herself grown old with the year, and wise as well.

The sea was a thousand miles away and still he dreamt of it day and night. She didn't exactly feel like singing but she could come to terms with it. She searched her mind for what should be done . . . If she could feel an answering pull, a long regret to match his own, it would be like climbing and sharing a rope and feeling from time to time the tug that kept you safe . . . that let you dream as much as you liked but kept you from slipping into space. That kept him from sailing around the world.

She had been very good with the music. It had broken her gifted mother's heart when Abby had married instead of going on and on to become the performer she herself had been. Whenever her mother recalled the stage her eyes were dark and bottomless pools. The excitement, the lights, the trains that were hurtling through the night, and the long call of the engine ahead, like a trumpet calling her into fame. She was rocked to sleep inside her berth, the womb from which she would wake into music and light, applause. However soundly now she slept, slept in the grave these twenty years, she would smile to dream that at seventy-one Abby was back at her scales again.

She would let him have his boats and books, a little of what he'd lost for her. And she would have what she'd lost for him. She had the blind man in to tune the old piano that stood in the hall. Together they moved it into the light. ("You could have waited for me," Max said.) It took the man three days to tune it. The moths had eaten most of the felts. And the cost was more than she liked to think, but the boats and books were hardly cheap.

And so they had finished the winter between them and then the spring and a summer and fall, each at separate ends of the rope. At times his saw would shatter her notes. But her music would lap at the ship he carved and give it a sea to sail upon. She hummed a lot. The opening bars of a Bach she was learning. Or a Schubert theme; he was easy to hum. It began to seem quite a natural thing, this life they lived, this rounding back when the children were past. This reaching back to take a direction each might have taken. The things regretted could be done after all. Not to perfection—no time for that—but certainly with pleasure. Certainly with that, and a sense of having sacrificed nothing, of having had both worlds. She rejoiced that it must be the same for Dave. He had seemed content.

So why had he moved to the end of the block? She was worn with the effort to understand. At last she saw, or she thought she saw, that he couldn't just leave her all at once without anything that came between. She supposed the hut was a step to the sea, a halfway house. He had simply moved from her to the the pier and then from the pier he would board his ship. The Widow's hut was the pier for him . . .

The Widow Wilson was new to the block. Abby had welcomed her with a call. She had been inside the Widow's house but never inside the hut behind. They had always called her the Widow Wilson since she had come two years ago. She had been widowed twice or thrice, or so it was said by those who knew. She had lived for years on the Florida Keys, but she was a drifter she often said. She was tall with hair the color of jet, a woman neither young nor old, preserved in her bracing self-regard with just a tang of slow ferment. Her yard in back was longer than theirs. They could easily see what she was about. They always spoke of her with a smile or with a tone that contained a smile: The Widow Wilson is beating her rug. The one with the storks? That's the one . . . The Widow Wilson is planting a bush. What kind of a bush? It has no leaves. No leaves at all? No leaves at all. A kind of litany it became whenever the Widow came up with them. She was anchored here for a while, she said, because of the grandson she called Jimbo, who was seventeen. And while he remained and she remained she studied the tongues of various nations that had won her favor. She was currently into Spanish and French. She studied them on alternate days. But on the Sabbath she rested, she said, and let it all sink sweetly in. She touched her breast. "I have it here." The Widow Wilson had ceased to be a cause for smiles. She was the ferryman on the bank that rowed Dave across to the other side.

For Abby the winter had settled in. She had settled into her own widowed state, a haunted state. Sometimes she was sure he was in the house, back in the room where his boats had been. Perhaps he had come for something he'd left. Or perhaps he had come home to stay. She seemed to hear the tap of his hammer nailing his maps against the wall . . . Sometimes while she played she would feel him behind her, listening, waiting for her to turn. And when she did he was never there. Sometimes at night he slept beside her. When she awoke his place was bare. Rarely she saw him out for a walk. From a distance he waved to her. None of it seemed real at all. There was about it an air of play, a kind of biding of their time as if to see what would happen next. By day her mind was thick with memories that jostled and murmured like birds that were bedding down in the trees. She played her music till weariness seized her and then she slept the dreamless night.

The children were bent on sackcloth and ashes. They dropped in now to rend their garments and look their shock at the state of things, Amy from a distant suburb, Max from his quarters near the store. From the first she would not discuss it with them. She understood it little more than they.

And here was Max with his silly tree intended to chide her once again. Or simply to be his primal scream.

She roamed the house with her cup of tea and could not avoid a glimpse of the tree. She wandered into the dining room and laid her cup beside the piano. She sat before it and stared into the slate-gray sky. The wind was tossing leaves from the trees. A squirrel's nest rocked in the swaying boughs. With her eyes shut she ran her fingers over the keys. They glided into the Raindrop Prelude. She saw Dave cling to the wheel of his ship, coughing his lungs up into the wind, the rain beating against his face. Everything went to his chest, of course. It seemed to her that he wanted to die, catch pneumonia and die at sea. Or split his ship on a treacherous reef. She could see it sundered like the tree . . .

But the worst of it wouldn't come to pass. He would simply get sick and come back home and sit around with a lump in his throat and a fever that came and went for months.

She finished the piece and dropped her hands. I think he will never go, she said.

It had been a month since he'd left the house. A month and almost seven days. The basket she kept beside the door was spilling over with mail for him. She was spilling over with need for him, with need to know he was wintering well. She had promised herself she would wait for him to come to her. But she told herself she was seventy-one and had no time to wait for him.

She put on her cape and wound a scarf around her hair. With his basket of mail she picked her way down the alley in back. Wind from the north was rushing at her. Clouds were boiling, fleeing south. Leaves were circling her like birds. The little brown hut stood back of the Widow Wilson's house, some ten or twelve feet to the rear of it, nesting among the leaves like a hen. The Widow professed to love it even more than she did her house. She was fond of calling it her adjunct, when she wasn't calling it her papoose. It was linked to the big house, also brown, by an arched umbilical cord of a walk. Between the two ran a drainage ditch and over its culvert the little walkway rose and fell. She called it her Japanese humpbacked bridge. It was bordered by lattice-work laced with vines, which rattled now in the frenzied wind. The Widow named them wisteria woven with muscadine, a union which had its charm for her. The blossoms of early summer, she said, passed on their purple to the grapes of fall. Her favorite color was purple, she said. Mauve, lilac, whatever, she said. "The color of love, I always say."

The drainage ditch, which the Widow Wilson called her brook, had not succumbed to the winter freeze. Abby heard its patter off to the left as she mounted the steps of the hut and knocked. Clutching her basket, muffled in cape, she felt like an aging Red Riding Hood. She all but turned and walked away.

Without delay Dave opened the door. He was looking well, she noted at once. Young, young, she thought with pride and then with sorrow. His stolid body could pass for younger. His skin was fresh. His hair that was once as yellow as sand, like a shore of the sea that was more to him now than all the land, had gone to white like a bone in the sun, but live it was and crisp and full. His eyes were still the color of sea, as filled with the dream as they had been fifty years ago.

He smiled as if he were shy of her, the way he had been when they told their names beside the lake so long ago. They had got their fishing lines in a tangle . . . And so their lines had always been. She held out the basket of mail in silence. He took it in some embarrassment. "I should have come for it," he said. But she saw that it would be hard for him to come and then to leave again. "You shouldn't be out in weather like this."

She was turning away, but he said, "Please stay."

After a moment she entered enough to let him lock outside the cold. It was very strange to be standing there like an alien child in an alien place. At least it was warm. A fire burned away on the hearth and made things shine all over the room. She saw at once that here was a brighter place to be than what he'd left. But small, small, too small for him. And full of the Widow Wilson's past. Her years, it seemed, on the Florida Keys. Her conch shells lined the mantel shelf. Her cowrie shells were strung in a festive loop by the door. And a glistening creature, mouth agape, looking very fresh from the sea and nailed as it were in a writhing leap, was mounted against the opposite wall.

But she did not care about the room. She searched his face, as if whatever had changed his heart must have changed his face. But it was the same face, solid with bone, the cheekbones wide, the skin of it tanned and faintly freckled, with lines about his eyes and brow, but the rest of it taut for his seventy years. She closed her eyes. For his face had become a forever face, one that the hands of her mind had known. One that her eyes didn't need to see and wanted somehow to keep that way.

He took her cape and gently unwound the scarf from her head. She held her breath when she felt his touch. Only his hands were wintered and old. The blow of a hammer had mangled one. With one the saw had bitten a bone, the one that was lashed with a purple scar. The lash of a whip it had seemed to her. She had loved his hands for the pain in them.

She was conscious that she, a year older than he, looked older still. Her hair, though yet with a measure of brown, had begun to thin. Each day she arranged it to hide the fact. More and more was her face a stranger. When she combed her hair before the glass, she had mastered a trick of creasing her eyes to let in only the face of her youth. Sometimes the face was her mother's face in the pictures made in the days of fame.

Her coming seemed to have humbled him. He tried to conceal it with throwing logs upon the fire and standing before it to watch them catch. She sat at one end of the sofa that faced it. The room was like a cove of the sea with its shimmer of light on stagnant water, with its mammoth shells each side of the hearth and the smaller ones lining the mantel above. Shapes of driftwood were here and there. She caught the faintest smell of brine. A ship's black anchor was fixed to the ceiling above the table where his maps were laid. A cord wove through a length of chain that swooped from wall and looped through anchor to shackle the hanging lamp above. A table of driftwood covered with glass was standing quite within her reach, and on it rested a bottled ship, larger than the one before.

She said to him in her warmest tone, "I'm glad you got another ship."

He half turned. "Vera gave it to me."

"Vera, is it?"

"She asked me to call her that," he said.

In the corner stood Max's tree, the other half of the one that stood before her hearth. It was lodged among the firewood. Its tinsel rippled with firelight. The cloven dove was smudged with ash. She could not take her eyes from it.

He turned to her. "I'm sorry you had to bother," he said, as if she were all of a stranger to him.

"I don't mind," she said, as if she were.

"I've given them all a change of address. You shouldn't be out in weather like this."

"I don't mind," she said.

They fell into silence.

A boy with a stocking cap pulled low came in with an armful of wood for the box. It was Jimbo, Abby saw at once. He had been around since his mother had gone in search of a job in the Windy City, as the Widow Wilson liked to call it. He was thin as a bean. He felled the tree when he dropped the wood. Then he propped it up among the logs. It fell again with a shower of tinsel. He tried once more while they watched in silence.

"Hello, Jimbo," Abby said.

"Hello," he growled through his clenched teeth. He pulled his stocking cap down to his chin and went straight out.

"Have I offended him?" Abby asked.

Dave gave a laugh. He seemed relieved by the brief intrusion. "No, he got in a fight and his jaw got broke. It's wired shut."

"I see," she said. "So how does he eat?"

"He sucks in soup and chocolate malts."

"I see," she said. "It must be awkward. Audible too."

"It is," he said.

She dropped her eyes to the bottled boat.

"Sometimes she invites me to dinner," he offered. "He inhales in the kitchen."

"I see," she said. She asked him after a silent moment, "Is there anything that you need from the house?" He seemed to consider and shook his head. "Then you're all right here? You have a kitchen." She supposed it was there behind the screen that was studded with pink and orange shells. She could hear the purr of refrigeration. "Are you eating well? Are you getting your fiber?"

He seemed to be touched, amused but troubled. "I'm fine," he said. "What about yourself?" He glanced at her and then away. "There's a phone, you know . . . You must call if you need anything at all."

The door from the passage flew open again. The Widow Wilson walked in upon them with a cake on a tray and a generous bottle. She bristled with hospitality. "Jimbo said you were here, lucky for me. I can't miss the chance for some *bonhomie*. My word for today. Today is French." She clattered in on her tall sandals and laid the tray down with the bottled boat. "You know that I'm studying Spanish and French. I refuse to hold one above the other, so I study them on alternate days. All languages are precious to me. When Jimbo is gone, which may be soon, I plan to travel again, you know, and I like to penetrate the culture. The culture is always dear to me." She was wearing green slacks, a white middy blouse, and a double loop necklace of small fat shells. Her face was long, as white and glistening as a pearl, with questioning brows. Her hair was copious and black. It swept from one ear, swirled up and back, then down to the other in a shining curl.

On her tray there were glasses, plates, and forks. She gave a shriek. "I forgot the knife." She dashed at once to the shell-studded screen and and slipped behind it to reappear wigwagging a knife. "Don't worry, Dave. I'll wash it, I promise."

She smiled at Abby. "I'm much at home in my little papoose." She sliced them fruitcake and poured them sherry. "If ever I build again, you know, which well may be, it well may be, I shall want nothing more than this little adjunct. Nothing to anchor me down again." She flourished her fork and dipped to her cake.

"This is good," said Abby, her lips in a smile.

"I bake it each year wherever I am. Every year on the Florida Keys—I lived on more than one, you know. All the Keys are precious to me—though there my neighbors found it strange."

The fire settled. The room shimmered and settled too.

The Widow gave a mysterious smile at a ribbon of tinsel beside her shoe. She lifted it gently by its end and tossed it gaily into the ash. "You may wonder why they found it strange. I think you would have to have known the Keys. Really, you would have to have known the sea." She glanced at Dave from under her brows. "It calls for something tart and sweet. And full of the wind. Key lime pie." She raised her eyes to the shells on the mantel. "Or a guava mousse." She was reverent. She raised her glass and then her voice. "*Votre santé,*" she toasted them. "*C'est la vie, mes amis.*"

Her eyes were dreaming into the flame. Dave swirled his sherry, his eyes on the fire, his face remote. And quietly Abby's astonishment grew that he was here in this clutter of shells, this bother of woman and firewood, with no more room for his books and maps than he'd had before. With no more peace . . . His models of ships were not about. Perhaps he had packed them all away. She studied his face. He wasn't there.

The Widow Wilson put down her glass and fluttered her hand. "I miss the Keys. I loved their warmth. And Christmas is such a time for warmth. Families gathered about the hearth . . ." Her smile took in the severed tree.

Abby felt her joy in the severed tree.

When she left, it had begun to snow. The wind had died. The Widow's brook drank chips of snow. Back at her house she plunged into the

Moonlight Sonata. Yes, she thought, he will surely go. I felt it there . . . She gave it up to her fingers at last. Yet even the music was not enough to say to herself what the hut had held.

Soon at the bank a great deal of money was in her account. When she learned of it her heart despaired.

The days passed. They were full of snow. She tried to retreat again into her youth. A sleighride once back into the hills. And the snow-muffled voices, her breath like milk, and her fingers so numb that it seemed she would never make music again. The scenes were touched with a fresh delight, but something would whirl them into the future, or whirl the future into them. The snow would be mixed with her honey-moon in a mountain resort. The snow-muffled voices would shift to the voices of Dave and Amy calling to her in the frosty air. Or Dave was building a fire for them, for her and Max, while they watched the snow melt off the wood and the flames hiss and all but sleep and wake again. The snow outside her window now was falling on all the snows she'd known.

There had been so little between her life in her mother's life and her life in Dave's. So little life that had been her own. When she tried to slip into her own, she was in her mother's past instead. She played the music her mother had played. She was rushing through night to the next concert hall, the long piano gleaming with light, the long moment while her fingers hovered, then struck the keys.

At night the lake was in her dreams. The white-limbed birches that circled the shore drew back like dancers to form a sea and the quiet waters foamed and raged. She would wake and will them calm again and will the sea to become the lake and will herself beside the lake unweaving her long dark braid for the sun, and Dave would be telling her of the sea. Sleeping and waking, she lived the sea.

She was glad when Amy dropped by.

"You came for shopping? How are my grandsons? Are they home from school?"

Amy stood in the hall. "They came last night." She walked past Abby to the living room and sat on the sofa to face the tree. She studied it briefly. "Max sent for me."

Abby followed her in and sat in the rocker to face her daughter. Nothing about the woman before her resembled the wistful girl she had been. Today she was wearing a sweater topped with a gray jumper. Summer and winter she wore a jumper. Her boys were grown and off at school, but still she had the look of a woman called from the kitchen, putting her apron by as she came, with not much time to give to you before she had to go back again. She had as little time for herself. Her hair was abandoned to graying, slightly untidy curls. Her shoes were scuffed. Her clothes were mussed. But those who found the look of her somewhat disarrayed were unprepared for the double-entry cast of her mind, the ledgered spirit of charity that organized holiday meals for the homeless and benefits for the children's home. The eyes were as sharply blue as her father's but older and shrewd as they took your measure. They rested upon her mother now. "Max sent for me," she said again.

Abby managed a smile. "I've set to music what he has to say. In E flat minor. I'll play it for us and then we can talk about Tim and Cal."

But Amy rose and circled the sofa and sat in the rocker made of wicker. It crackled like flame. "Mama, it's hard to give you a lecture."

"It's hard to take one," Abby said.

But her daughter was staring down a tunnel with the tree at the end of it, Abby could see. "I know Max has spoken. I'll put it my way . . . There are times in a marriage . . . there are times in my own when I've wanted to call the whole thing off, just go my way. This is hard to say. I'm fond of Nick, but there hasn't been all that much for years. He doesn't feed me. Oh, I don't mean food, for god's sake no, I don't mean groceries. I mean he doesn't nourish me." She tore her eyes away from the tree.

Abby had listened with the pillows of the chair lumped into her back. "Are you telling me that you're leaving Nick?"

Amy ran her fingers through her graying curls and set the chair into a crackle. "I'm certainly not! I'm telling you just the opposite of that. I'm telling you I've stuck it out and will stick it out. Because I have children. As you have children."

"My children are grown and on their own. I've finished with them except to love them. And that I do. I want them to have a happy life. And if they don't it makes me sad."

In the silence that followed she felt how Amy searched her mind for the file marked Mother and tossed it aside. "And that is all you have to say?"

"I'm afraid it is, but I'm glad you came. So how is Tim and how is Cal?"

Amy stood with a protest from the chair. Her jaw was set. "Well, Mama, if that's the way it is, well, we won't be able to make it for Christmas. It would be too painful for all of us."

"Not for me . . . You must do what you think is best for yourself. If you've made up your mind, you can take home a box of the gifts I've wrapped."

Amy waited where she stood and took the box without a word. At the door she turned. "Get rid of that tree. It's obscene, Mama. Have you any idea what you've done to Max?"

Abby searched her daughter's face for a hint of the charity others enjoyed. "Drop in on your father before you leave."

Through the window she watched her daughter go. She watched cars pass in a flutter of snow. She watched their tracks fill up with snow. She was heavy with empty days to come, as if with child.

She decided not to think about Christmas, not to give it another thought. When the Widow Wilson learned from Dave that the children would not be coming this year, it would be like her to have him over the humpbacked bridge and give him a cozy holiday meal, with Jimbo sucking it up in the kitchen. She would end perhaps with a Key lime pie, tart and sweet and full of the wind, to give them just a taste of the sea. And then she would load a plate for Abby, bear it, mincing, through the snow, and knocking sweetly she would say, "*Bonjour, ami*" or "*Buenos días*," whatever her lesson for the day.

Abby threw her tree into the trash. She played her music for the rest of the day.

The mail kept piling up for Dave, papers and books that she thought could wait. But then came letters from a Capt. Trent, a series of them. So she took them down on a misting day, and there was Dave with an eager look when he saw the lot. He was actually getting a deeper tan and a weathered skin and a distant look in his sea-blue eyes. Or so it seemed to her he was. The Widow Wilson called from within, "Come in, *amigo, por favor.*"

"Come in," said Dave and apologized for the trouble she took. "I've given this man my new address. I don't understand. I've given it."

She stepped inside, but just to say that Max would come for the Christmas meal. His silence told her the fact was hers. He had sailed away from Christmas Day. A kind of mist enveloped them now, as if it had followed her through the door. It dimmed the face he turned to her. It muted the words she tried to speak.

The Widow Wilson presided here. She had slipped into the vacancy. Free of the mist, she was sharp and clear. She stood with towels looped over her arm, regally stood like a consort queen supplying order and lively care and a leavening for the soggy day. A tray of food was before the hearth. She laid her burden of linens down to glide to the couch against the wall, and with a practiced sleight of hand she stripped the sheets from under the spread and wound them into a snowy muff through which she plunged her braceleted arm. She was wearing slacks and a middy blouse with an anchor appliquéd to the breast. And in the lobe of either ear was a small white coral gull in flight.

A fire was burning in the grate. The shells in the screen seemed to purr with light. And the ocean creature nailed to the wall writhed in the shadows that flickered there.

"Are you ready for Christmas?" the Widow asked. The firelight danced in her lacquered hair. "I can't help thinking," she mused aloud, "how it would be, a Christmas at sea. Can't you just see the spray at the porthole looking for all the world like snow? Does it snow at sea? I wonder, now. Of course it didn't off the Keys." She turned to Abby. "I lived for years on the Florida Keys. I have the sea in my heart and bones." With a hand that protruded from the muff she waved at the anchor fixed to the ceiling and dipped to the anchor fixed to her breast. "The anchor isn't my thing at all. Whenever I've had to drop my own, as I've had for a while to do it for Jimbo, it's always been against my wish. *A bon voyage* is the life for me."

Dave was silent, into his letters. A gleam of tinsel came from the tree. It was lying prone in the box of wood. "I'll just be on my way," said Abby. She passed the table spilling over with maps, continents of a shifting green with seas between that were fathoms deep, so deep-down blue they took her breath. The deeper the blue, the deeper the sea.

"If you must," said the Widow, smiling. "*Hasta la vista,* my words for the day." She waved goodbye from the snowy muff.

The house was dusk after all the pulsing light of the hut. Abby played her music and could not stop. When the hours passed into an early night, she played in the dark and went to bed without her supper. She lay and waited for sleep to come. The wind had risen. She heard it back in the trees again, stripping the last of their summer away, blowing her summer away as well. Her years with Dave were blowing away. The fine young years and the later ones that were crisp and warm as apples ripening in the sun. These final days, most precious to her, that might have glowed with a golden light . . . the Widow Wilson was gifted with them. This was the hardest thing to bear.

In the chill of the night she blew on the coal of her dying dream to make their division a noble thing. A fork in the river of their lives when each would wander a different field, when the current of each would channel its course, till they came together somewhere beyond to pool their memories of various banks and flow the richer into the sea. But the Widow Wilson diminished it. She reduced it all to the sly glance, to the middy blouse with the anchor attached and stripping the sheets before their eyes.

She did not walk to the hut again. She would let him drift away from her like a ship that has gently slipped its moorings. She let the mail for him pile up. After a while it would cease to come.

But Christmas came, and with it Max on the stroke of twelve. With a show of bluster he stood in the hallway rubbing his hands. The green plaid scarf embraced his ears that were rimmed with pink. He unwound the scarf from about his neck. He made an elaborate gesture of it, not meeting her eyes, not saying a word but making sounds to support the cold, making the weather seem worse than it was. He shrugged his coat into her waiting arms.

"Do you want your present now?" he asked. "It's in the car." He seemed embarrassed and ill at ease, anxious to put the day to rest.

She scanned his face. "Let's wait," she said. She wanted to say, Let's wait forever. When one was young it was hard to wait, but later on, the occasion seemed to require much. She led him straight to the dining room.

He circled and straddled the piano bench. "I don't mind saying I find you hard to select for now." She smiled at him. He gazed at her sadly.

"I made a mess of it," he confessed. "I ended up with a thing from the store. It's fairly big. And nothing you want. That's why I left it in the trunk."

"Don't worry about it." She brought him a little wine in a glass. "We'll have some wine and then we'll eat. I've made you something you've always liked. Macaroni with tons of cheese. And maybe next week we'll give our gifts."

He looked relieved. She patted his hand. "We're fine, Max. We're really fine. I think I'll turn up the heat a bit. Sometimes I like it to get too hot, then run outside to be glad it's cold."

He sipped his wine and relaxed for her. He watched her dot the table with silver and plates of food. Then he ate with absorption. He was down in the food, the way she was sometimes down in her music. Down so far it was hard to return. He was helping himself to far too much. And when he had surfaced, cornering the crumbs of her apple pie, he raised his eyes. "I thought he might come. Did you ask him to?"

She waited a bit. "I told him you would be coming today."

"Amy might at least have showed . . . You haven't eaten a thing, you know." He pushed his plate away at last. "I'm glad I never got married," he said. "If this is what . . ." He could not finish. Through the dollhouse windows she saw his tears.

She rose and took him in her arms. "It will be all right. You'll see, my dear."

"I could move in and look after you."

"Of course not, Max, I'll be fine. You'll see."

He drew away and took off his glasses to wipe his eyes. He blew his nose. There were lines in his face she had never seen until this day. He circled the room. He rattled the change in his pocket a while. "Did you get him a gift?"

"I did," she said.

"What is it?" he asked.

She hesitated and then she smiled. "It's a wonderful sweater to wear at sea."

"And that's all? You used to get him a dozen things."

She gave a little rueful laugh. "You think a dozen would bring him back? The one I got is costly, Max. And it will stand for all the rest . . . I wanted to bless the waves for him."

He was looking at her with astonishment.

"The way the bishops used to do. Before the ships went out to sea."

"You want him to go?"

She waited and turned her face away. "If he can go, he may come back before it's too late." She scarcely knew what she meant by it. "And if he can't, he may just move from us farther away. To the coast next time, to be near the boats. I want him to have the courage to go."

Max ducked his head and prowled the room. "I think it's really that woman," he said. "He's lusting after that damn fool woman."

"Really, Max . . ."

"Well, have you seen her make up to him? The outfits she wears? Ready and waiting to climb aboard. Doesn't his being there get to you?" He struck the table with his fist. "That kid around with the wired jaw!"

She did not answer him at once. "It should be a sad but beautiful thing. A worthy thing, with dignity. She doesn't seem to belong in this . . ."

"This plot?" he said. "This mad sea tale? Maybe she's right at home in it. I'll bet she sings him a chantey at night and plies him with grog before the fire."

She ignored his excess. She dropped to her chair. "I'm afraid I haven't coped with her well."

He stared at her. "You'd do far better to cope with him. I find him even more absurd. An old man taking off to sea."

"Not that," she said. "It's a dream of his for all his life. We cannot call his life absurd."

"Then why is he down there? Tell me that."

She waited. She wanted to do her best. "I think it's a place on the way to the sea. A place he will find it easy to leave. A place that's too absurd to mourn . . . A halfway house while he waits for spring."

"I made him show me the tub he's chartered, a picture of it. And a snap of the pilot, beard and all, a murderer's face. He'll rob him and throw him overboard."

"Part of him doesn't want to go . . ." She turned away. "I pray he will. Once I stood in the way of his dream, and now I must help him get on with it."

Max blew his nose and fogged his glasses. He polished them with the hem of his shirt. "I don't understand either one of you."

"Where is it written you must?" she asked.

Then he was gone to work off his meal. To bowl, he said, if an alley was open. She left the table just as it was. She went to her music, searching the notes, becoming the sea. She blessed the waves, and blessed herself.

Now at last she would go to the hut. But a weariness came over her, like a wave from the music, a wave she had made. She wandered into the living room and lay on the sofa to rest a bit. At once she slept and began to dream.

In her dream she had already reached the hut. When Dave let her in, his face was strange. His lips were smiling, his eyes blue ice. The fire had died. She was very cold. She heard herself: "I came to say we are married still. And that if you take this woman to bed it is very wrong . . ." She became aware that the Widow Wilson was behind the screen. She could not finish and turned away. She saw the gleam of the tree in the box. "Would you care if I should do the same?" She turned to see him smiling at her. "Whatever gives you pleasure," he said. She could scarcely breathe for the weight of sorrow.

She woke up weeping. She was very cold. She lay quite still, rejecting the dream with all her soul. An unworthy dream. Unworthy of her, unworthy of him. Though perhaps not so of the woman who lurked behind the screen. She got up at last and slipped her cape about her shoulders and tied the scarf about her head. By the clock it was three in the afternoon. She got his gift from the bedroom where it had been for weeks.

She picked up her music, an armful of it, and went out the back. The wind was sour with stale smoke and cold ash. She tasted it in her mouth at once. My life, she thought, has gone to smoke. The fire of it has gone to smoke. No shape to it, all drift and gray. The boxwoods that bordered her walk were trembling, as if they knew and feared the worst. Dead leaves like pigeons were refuged in them. Roses gone to tangle and stem were bobbing beside the wooden fence. Above the Widow Wilson's house birds were blown about like kites. From one of the houses a carol came.

When he opened the door and saw her gift his eyes were stricken, almost angry, then resigned. "I knew it would come to this," he said. "I looked for yours but it didn't work."

"I know," she said. "I understand." She laid her music on the seat of a chair—she couldn't think why she had brought it along—and held out the box she had for him. "This is really something for going away."

He did not want to take it from her. He stifled a cough. The winter had gone to his chest at last. "You shouldn't be out in the wind," he said. When his chest was bad he would always speak as if it were hers.

"I'm not anymore. So open it."

At last he let it be given to him. She took off her scarf and then her cape. "May I sit for a moment?"

"Please," he said. A smudge of ink was on his face. His table was littered with charts and maps spilling their seas upon the floor. The deeper the blue, the deeper the sea . . . The fire had almost died in the grate, as in her dream. The room was cool. She could not avoid a glance at the screen where her dream had placed the Widow Wilson.

She was filled with a need to talk with him. Simple words about simple things. "Have you eaten?" she asked.

"I wasn't hungry." He coughed once more. She knew that tonight she would lie awake and his cough would be borne to her on the wind. She would hear it later far out at sea.

He laid her box on the mantel where it nudged the shells. He began to pace before the hearth. He seemed to her like a man who is trapped, not one who is free to find his dream.

Trapped in his dream, it came to her. But perhaps he chafed at the long delay. He waited for spring. He felt time running out for him. As it is, she thought. Dear God, it is. She was in his body pacing with him, feeling how time ran out for him and for herself and for them both. She was feeling how empty her bed had been. How empty his had been as well. He was sleeping now on the narrow couch against the wall. And this was only a step away from one narrower still that rocked at sea. And this was only a step away from one narrower still . . . She stopped herself.

He coughed again. She knew the sweet and bitter smell of the syrup he never wanted to take but waited for her to measure and bring. Fear for him gathered and struck at her with a violence that left her trembling. The day had suddenly been too long. She hungered for night to let her sleep. She calmed herself enough to speak. "Please open the box," she said to him. She prayed that the Widow would leave them in peace, grant them a little space to be.

He tore off the wrapping to get her gifting over and done. He lifted the cover and saw the sweater. He did not take it out of the box. He only continued to look at it.

"It's something to wear at sea," she said. "It comes from Ireland. They're made on the Aran Islands there. The wool isn't washed, so the oil keeps out the spray and rain . . ."

He would not lift his eyes to her.

"It smells a little like sheep, I'm afraid."

After a while he spoke as if he were seeing the words. "The way it's knit . . . Each family had a different way. When a man is lost and a piece of this is washed ashore . . . they will know who it is gone down, they say."

She looked away from him in pain. "I forget how many books you read. I didn't know . . . If that is so, it's a good thing."

They could not speak. After a moment she said again. "It's a good thing." For the moment they seemed to cling in mourning. Fragile as glass their spirits were. If the Widow Wilson should enter now, they would break and shatter before her eyes.

He laid her gift beside the hearth. The vein in his temple sprang to life. The embers burnished his wounded hands. He straightened and stared at the anchor that hung above his maps. "You must understand that all these years I have been asleep. My life has been a sleep, a dream. A fine dream with the children and you . . . yet still a dream. If I don't go now, I shall die in my sleep . . . But when the ship is under me, when I feel it move, I shall wake and live."

She told herself, No, the ship is a dream. Like a child in the womb he made it sound. He seemed to have memorized the words and saved them up for her to hear. Said them until they became a poem and after that they were true for him. Poems had always been true for him, turning his dreams into things to touch. She said at last, "And all this time you slept in my arms."

He did not reply.

"Shall I sleep, then, while you're awake?"

"No," he said firmly, "you have your music."

"My music is dreaming" was all she could say. A truer thing she had never said. The music had sung her mother awake. But Abby had left it back, back in her dreaming youth, when Dave had waked her out of the dream. And now it was all that was left for her. She was seeing the sheaf of it on the chair. "I want you to go to sea," she said. "You're young and strong as you ever were. I want you to go as far as you can. The world is round and will bring you back." Bring you home, she wanted to say.

He seemed to be lost in the fireshine. She gave him up to the sea at last, knowing he wasn't as she had said, either young or strong enough to go, knowing that if he came back at all he would be weary and old and sick, wind haunted and wave spent. And she would be left with a pillar of salt to care for till the day he died or she died, whichever it was. But still she wanted him to go. All her will was gathered up and loosed like winds upon his ship.

The fire roused and shimmered over the cowrie shells. She rose and walked to the box in the corner. She lifted the severed slice of pine and laid it gently across the embers. The tinsel shone; the drying needles caught and flamed. "We want the same," she said to him. "You'll be at sea and I'll be here but closer to you than I am today. For nothing will keep my mind from you, my dreams from you . . . my heart from you."

She lifted the music from the chair. "You call this mine but it isn't mine. This is the house I live in now, but it isn't mine." She laid it among the flaming boughs. "The music makes me dream," she said. "I want to be awake with you."

The pages curled, the notes danced, the sap rose with the fervor of spring, the tree sang.

She seemed to have taken his words from him or thrust them down too far to reach. Then he turned and with a thrust of his hand he swept the bottled ship from the table and laid it down in the midst of the song. The flames curled about the glass. It shuddered a moment like water and burst. For a time the ship was afloat in it, in molten glass and running sap. Till the sails flamed.

Her voice shook. "How can we think we have time enough left to play games?" she asked. "Games are for children with plenty of time . . . I cannot bear it to be a game."

"It isn't a game. It was never a game."

"It will be a game unless you go. You must go to make it a part of our life. The way our life was going to be. It will have a strange and sorrowful end, but meant to be."

He backed to the sofa and sat to watch. The ship was in flames, but he had not told her what it meant. She stood there looking down at him, and she seemed to catch the glint of his tears. "Tell me not to go," he said.

"Nobody gives me the right," she said.

"I give you the right."

But she shook her head.

"All the years with me gives you the right."

She could not speak.

He smiled at the fire and went on smiling. It seemed to her he would smile forever. He had been so far away at sea. The voyage home was long for him. She could hear the wind in the eaves of the hut. Down through the chimney it puffed the fire into a rage till it roared like the sea, then gentled it. He dropped his head to the pillow behind. "There's an old ship . . . has lost its rudder."

"Not old." She could only whisper it. "A fine brave ship. Not old to me."

The wind was whispering in the pine. "Then what?" he said. "Give me a name. An old boxcar . . . has got derailed."

The fire was burning into her face and down her throat and into her breast. She would not reach out a hand to him lest, seeing it, he turn and flee. She spoke in the low, remembering voice with which she had given her past away to Max and Amy when they were small. The voice of her mother giving her daughter the vanished world that glowed in the dark. "Whatever happened to trains?" she said. "When I was a girl . . . when I was a girl there was nothing sadder than trains at night, away in the distance yearning away. I always wanted to comfort them . . . Give them whatever they cried to have."

"Help them back on the rails again."

Not for the world would she turn to him. The past was all that was safe for her. She was gone back and boarding the train. She was her mother rushing through night to the long piano shining like silk, no, shining like flame in the lights of the stage . . . And then she was Abby rushing out of her mother, hurtling into her own sweet life.

He said, "You were being your mother again. I can always tell it whenever you are . . . And now you're back in yourself again. Now you're the Abby I married," he said.

"You will always hold me to blame for that."

She waited for him.

". . . Just hold you," he said.

They were starting again beside the lake. He drew her down and into his arms. They smelled to her of the burning pine. The tree, steeped in its wine, sang . . .

The Widow Wilson stood in the doorway bearing a tray. It contained two glasses and a carafe. A sprig of holly was pinned to her collar; her bell-bottomed trousers were banded with red. Her amazed eye caught the blackened ship among the boughs. It caught the embrace.

"This room is occupied," said Abby. "*Occupé, occupado,* whatever," she said.

In the Widow Wilson's astonished eye a dream died. She shut them away. She shut them in.

The Pearl Sitter

That was the way spring came to the city, all mucked up with money and soot and odors sunned alive in the alleys, and a feeling Richard would always have that things should be better than he knew they were.

Richard was forty-eight and a broker. Most of his life had been ticker tape. It was stuttered out on a paper ribbon. Each day he let it glide through his hand and watched it coil and snarl in the can. At the end of the day it was dumped in the trash.

He had the slightly covert look of those who think a great deal about money. Even his one diversion was money. He was ambushed into collecting coins. His uncle had left him an opium-scented Manchurian coat and in the pocket he had found a doubloon. The deceased had been keen on such little distortions as leaving a coin wrapped up in a coat.

His departure left Richard with no relations except for the aunt, Henrietta, by marriage. On the first of the month like a bill collector she got in touch. Wherever he was she flagged him down with an invitation for supper at six. The time and the place were always the same; in fact, he had marked it on his calendar. But she wouldn't call it a regular thing. She wanted them both to be surprised. His uncle, she said, had been fond of making adventures for her, and now she must make them for herself. She always said, "I'm unsteady, you know, since your uncle passed. I can't seem to find my center of gravity." And then she issued her invitation as if he must come to keep her from toppling.

He didn't mind, for he liked his aunt. He had always preferred her to his uncle, who had been in his lifetime a bit of a bounder. She set a good table, she was really a sport, and best of all she seemed to adore him. They shared a need to be fond of someone. But mostly they shared a concern for her stocks, which he managed for her with a warm devotion. At the end of the evening she would smile at him with a hapless sigh. "Find someone, Richard." Then her eyes would tear at the thought of his uncle, who had passed from this earth a decade ago.

"I have you, Henrietta."

"Find someone sweet."

He always left with that grave imperative on her lips.

As soon as he had quitted her driveway he forgot all about it, or so he said. He remembered instead that he had his coins. The best ones, the ones that were really of value, he didn't allow himself to touch. It reduced their value if ever so slightly the edges were worn.

In the course of his business Richard dispensed a good deal of advice. The best advice he took for himself. It followed then as the night the day that he owned some stocks, a handful of bonds, and rented a box from the safest bank. At least once a week he was into his box, changing things there as the market changed. He struck up a friendship of sorts with Miss Doyle, who guarded the boxes and kept the key. It amused him to find her a sleeping dragon whose wrath he was careful not to arouse. Without her key his own was nothing, but that is the way of a bank with a box.

"I must trouble you again," he would say with regret.

She would smile her forgiveness. "It's what I'm for." With a generous flourish she would wave her key before she preceded him to his box. She had iron-gray hair in iron waves. She patted and pinched and crimped her hair as if she were fondling and grooming a pet.

He usually went into his box after lunch, but he had occasion this day of spring to enter it at a quarter of ten. His particular bank had placed its boxes at the end of a corridor. To the right was the vault with a small antechamber devoid of decor where employees would pause on their way to the vault, the holy of holies, to make obeisance or sort things out that had just been removed, an area naked to the eye of Miss Doyle. It was blocked from the hall by a wall waist high, and a quaint iron gate kept it safely locked from the snooping client with time on his hands. Richard never, of course, had time on his hands. While he briefly lunched or strolled to his box, the market was changing for better or worse. But on this day he was caught by the sight of a woman sitting in the sanctuary. Her pose and appearance were so at odds with her stark surroundings that he paused for a moment to take her in.

She was a young woman of voluptuous build. Her features were softly formed, like a child's. Her hair was fair, the color of honey, swept from her face and up from her neck, the neckline widely oval and low. Most striking to him was the skin of her throat and chest, creamy, translucent, but faintly flushed as if warm to the touch. On it there rested a string of pearls. Or rather, they floated, for her breathing was measured, entirely discernible. The shell-like skin overlaid with the pearls was thrown into relief by the black of her dress. He stood for fully a minute to watch her. She gave not the slightest notice of him as almost mechanically she turned the pages, scarcely pausing to scan them at all.

He went to his box. He was trailed by Miss Doyle with her precious key. He casually asked, "Who is the woman inside the gate? . . . Like Whistler's mother," he thought to add, in case Miss Doyle had noted how long he had lingered to look.

She smiled with indulgence. "You noticed," she said with an arch little glance. "She is hired, you know, to sit with the pearls."

Then, seeing how really puzzled he was, she graciously undertook to explain. "We have clients who keep their pearls in the bank. They rent a box. And of course you've heard . . . well, the saying is that they have to be worn to stay beautiful."

"No, I hadn't heard."

She took his key and thrust in her own. There was something erotic, he thought, in the gesture. "It may not be true. I really can't say." She opened his box and removed her key from the door with a flourish. "This is one of the services the bank provides. We hire a woman to sit with the pearls on a regular basis. She is screened, of course. And bonded, oh yes." She lingered a moment, tossing her key and fondling her hair. She said with a smile, "The skin, they say, adds a certain lustre . . . or preserves the lustre of the finest pearls. Something in the chemistry of the skin they say . . . We try to get someone with suitable skin." He saw that her hand had strayed to her throat.

"I see," he said. "And what kind would that be?"

"Beautiful," she said without any pause. And then he was sure she had seen how long he had stood at the gate.

When he left, the woman was still with the pearls. Under the watchful eye of Miss Doyle he gave them only a passing glance.

But he could not erase the indelible scene. It haunted his days and invaded his dreams. He was restless that night and for nights to come. The touch of his coins did not console him. And the sight of robins scratching for food in the barely greening grass of the park filled him with longing he could not explain.

He waited for a week and then he returned at a quarter of ten. There was no one sitting behind the wall. He reflected how scanty a knowledge he had of the ways of pearls or the owners of pearls and the craving for lustre, so great it seemed that human flesh could be bought to preserve it. More to his purpose, he could not imagine how frequent a contact the pearls required. There was something exciting, even enchanting, in the thought that science had found for this purpose no substitute for the throat of a woman (as indeed it had found none at all for the oyster). His aunt had pearls, a gift from his uncle, which she wore on occasion and of which she was fond of extolling the virtures. They kept alive her most ardent memories. He doubted that lustre had entered her mind.

Although he had no real occasion for it, he entered his box the following week at a quarter of ten, and then again on the week after that. On each of these trips he saw no sign of a woman with pearls. He lingered with his box in industrious show to justify to Miss Doyle the trip, her matey words, her wave of the key. But more, to demonstrate to himself that he had not lost his wits in the spring.

The following week he had his reward. His dreams came alive when he saw her there, turning her pages as if indeed she had never left. Miss Doyle was opening someone's box. He could hear her voice at the end of the corridor. Without any shame he stared at the woman behind the wall. Again she gave no sign of his presence. He was gratified that nothing had changed. The same serene, half-drooping pose with arms relaxed on the arm of the chair, eyes cast down to the page she turned. Even the magazine was the same, on the cover the scene of a girl with a dog. The pearls were arranged in precisely the oval he had recalled. The flush of her skin, the gentle ebb and flow of her breath. The air of a mermaid newly risen, with pearls from the deep caught up in her breast.

And then Miss Doyle bore down upon them. As he followed he said in his heartiest tones, "Why must you keep this young woman locked up?"

She turned to smile. "Well, of course it's the policy of the bank. It discourages conversation, you know. It's rather an agreement we have with the bondsman."

"But couldn't," he countered, still jovial, "but couldn't a customer leap the wall and snatch the pearls? Or is she wired to an alarm?"

She smiled at him thinly. "We have taken precautions." He had gone too far.

He laughed and shrugged and gave to the box his entire attention. Whereupon Miss Doyle discreetly withdrew.

By entering the bank on random days at random hours to make a deposit or cash a check—he could at a glance observe the enclosure— he discovered the woman at other times. On Tuesdays at half past nine she was there. Then, so far as he could determine the matter, she sat with two different strands of pearls. And she sat with each regularly once a month.

Armed with his knowledge he timed his visits accordingly. He found he was looking forward to days when he would enter his box at last and counting as lost the days he would not. Perhaps not lost but savorless, though after a while he counted them lost. He found that he thought of her constantly. The sales he arranged, the advice bestowed, were merely the frame for a throat and breast that cradled the glimmer of lustrous pearls.

Something about the line of her chin and the soaring sweep of her honey-light hair recalled a woman he once had known, one whose loss he had lived to regret. And he could not say if he sought the echo or a surrogate for a withered dream.

The days of spring were longer and sweeter. Safe in its iron fence by the bank, the gingko tree was unfolding.

The hours grew soft with light that gentled the brick and stone he called his world. Birds were tumbling out of the sky. One night he allowed himself to hold and stroke the best of his coins. He had never done such a thing before.

The following morning Henrietta called to say that she was expecting him. She sighed a little into his ear. "Spring is bad since your uncle passed. You remember he passed away this month."

"I remember," he said, though he hadn't at all.

In the afternoon he cashed a check and accosted Miss Doyle. "I was wondering. My aunt has a valuable string of pearls that she wants me to put in the bank for her."

"Of course," she said. "I'll arrange for a box."

"And another thing. I happened to mention the woman who sits here with the pearls. She was really quite taken with having them worn . . . I wonder if you could arrange for this, too."

Her eyes came to rest on him just for a moment. "It is really a tedious thing to arrange. We have to have them appraised, you see. And if your aunt should want them to wear, when we get them back it has to be done all over again."

"She rarely does," he assured her warmly.

"Well . . . I'm sure it could be arranged."

That night as planned he went to his aunt's. Over an excellent rack of lamb he offered her the best of himself. She was soft and rather sweetly crumpled. Her hair rejoiced in another change. Tonight it was tinted a gold champagne and arranged in an effervescent style. It almost seemed to bubble for him as she gently nodded her full approval. She loved to hear him talk of her stocks, and she understood not a word he said. "Oh, I do wish Henry could hear you now. He would have understood, you know. You're so much like him, Richard dear"—a disclosure which gave him small delight.

Over the coffee in red Ming cups he brought it up. "What have you done with your pearls?" he asked. "I couldn't recall if you have them safely put in the bank." He knew that she kept them beside her bed.

She looked the tiniest bit alarmed.

"We get these reports of robberies . . ."

"You do?" she said. "In your line of work?"

"Oh, yes," he said. "People decide to sell their jewels and put the money into stocks and bonds, and then they find the jewelry is missing."

"I wouldn't sell them." She was firm. "Your uncle gave them to me, you know."

He didn't answer how well he knew. He sipped his coffee and settled back to let her tell him the tale of the pearls. She liked to tell him. She liked to tell anyone who would listen. Once a year, at the charity ball when she wore the pearls, he would come upon her closely surrounded by a group of those who hadn't heard the tale.

Now her voice assumed the special tone—a soft, remembering, bell-like note, which seemed to echo her sweetest years. "We were going to be married, your uncle and I, but your uncle was given a bridge to build on one of those islands, part of Hawaii. We said we would put the wedding off. But then we thought how long it would be, and we made up our minds to let the trip be our honeymoon . . ."

She smiled at the tiny red cup in her hand.

"We weren't together as much as we liked. Henry was gone for most of the day. Away in those places . . . they were very wild, really a jungle . . . with all those primitive natives around, trying to get them to build a bridge. He said they didn't want the bridge. But once he took a whole day off. We rented a car and drove for miles till we came to a cove at the end of the island. The flowers, Richard, you wouldn't believe. And all around us divers for pearls. Some of them girls. Straight from the rock. So graceful they were, and full of laughter. We watched them and sipped a wonderful drink your uncle had brought. And after a while one of the divers—he looked like a god, all gold with sun—came out of the waves and climbed straight up the rock to me. Why is he coming to me? I thought. He knelt at my feet and laid an oyster on the grass before me. 'Henry,' I said, 'what on earth does he mean?' 'He wants you to open the oyster, my dear.' So I knelt and opened that oyster up. Inside was a beautiful, perfect pearl. Of course your uncle had put it there and hired the diver to bring it to me as if it had just come out of the sea. He liked to make adventures for me. 'This is your wedding gift,' he said."

She lowered her cup and touched each eye with the hem of her napkin. He waited for her to dream a little.

"I was so afraid I was going to lose it, I took it with me wherever I went. Henry said I should have a ring, but I didn't want to leave it with them. I never really trusted the natives . . . And then . . ." she said.

Her voice was braving the words to come, the euphemism she always employed for the time when his uncle had gone astray. First one woman and then another. "Your uncle drifted for a little while . . ."

It must have been for a good five years. And then one day he had given it up. Richard had always secretly thought that a jealous husband who owned a gun had accomplished his uncle's return to the fold. (Surely she must have omitted the drift when she told her tale at the charity ball.) He had drifted back with a strange request. "Let me borrow your pearl," he had said.

Now they were back in the tale again. Richard stretched his legs beneath the table. He had heard it so many times before that he could, if he liked, have set it to music.

"At first I hated to give it up. It was full of the sweetest memories for me. But Henry pressed me and promised it back. I couldn't dream what he wanted it for." She paused to savor her own surprise. "He returned my pearl with fifty others exactly like it. 'I love you,' he said, 'fifty times more than I did when I gave you the single pearl.' I was overcome, but also the tiniest bit I was sad, because I couldn't tell which pearl was the first, the one the diver had laid at my feet."

"They're lovely," he said, as he always did at this point in the tale. Indeed, she waited for him to say it.

"But you know," she went on, "after a while I could pass the necklace through my hands and the very first pearl would speak to me. There was something about it a little different. Perhaps the feel. It's hard to say . . . But you can't convince me I don't know."

He said to her now, "You really should let me put them in a box at the bank for you."

"I keep them safe."

"As safe as you can, which is not safe enough. I know how much they mean to you."

"But Richard, I wear them."

"Whenever you want them I'll get them out. Give me a ring. No trouble at all. I'm always going into my box, and yours will be in a box nearby. Besides, it will give me an excuse to see you."

After a time he persuaded her. She got them and put them into his hands. He smiled at her. "Do you have a bill of authentication . . . something that says the pearls are real?"

"I know what it means," she gently chided. "But how could you ask? Of course they're real."

"I know they are. It's for the bank."

She thought a moment. "Well, I do have a piece of paper that says it. It's signed by the dearest friend we had. A wonderful man and a wonderful jeweler. He was the one who found the pearls. One at a time, Henry said. It took him almost a year to do it."

Amazed at his cunning, Richard left. Yet he told himself it was all for the best. The pearls were safer kept in the bank.

The following day he rented a box. Miss Doyle performed her ritual. "Have you arranged for the sittings?" he asked. He laughed a little. "I really don't know what else to call them."

She patted her hair. "I believe I have her down for a Wednesday once a month at eleven o'clock. I will have a key to get them for her. You understand I must have a key? And someone else must have a key. The bank requires dual control."

"Of course," he said.

"I'm afraid the sittings must be postponed. Our appraiser is taken ill with the flu. I always say it's worse in the spring."

He was ready for her. "Perhaps for the moment this will do." He drew from his wallet the slip of paper his aunt had produced. She looked at it with large distaste. Then she sighed and said it might do for the moment.

"My aunt," he said, "would dislike a delay. But there's one other thing. My aunt insists that I meet the woman who will wear her pearls. She can't bear the thought of an utter stranger . . . you understand. A gift from my uncle who has passed away."

She frowned and looked down the corridor. "That is really against our policy. The bank has felt that matters like this must be kept impersonal."

He nodded gravely. "I quite agree. But my aunt insists. Perhaps an exception . . ."

She pursed her lips and pushed her hair. "I must ask the young woman if she consents."

"Of course," he said.

Miss Doyle suspected him, he was sure. Though it wasn't clear just what it was she suspected him of. Their easy relation had subtly changed. Darkness gathered about her brow. When he said, "I must trouble you yet again," she failed to reply, "It's what I'm for." She seemed, as she twisted her key in his lock, to say she was for a number of things.

Now for a time she left him hanging . . .

He fell back into his ticker-tape life, but he felt he was pacing inside his mind. He arranged his coins like a string of pearls, counting exactly fifty-one, mentally begging his aunt's forgiveness. Forgiveness for what? For keeping her treasures safer than ever? No, he thought. For wresting them from her with cunning and stealth.

The following Wednesday Miss Doyle was on his line at the office. Her voice was chilled, as if she were pouring it out of a thermos and into a glass upon her desk. "Miss Medlock is here to sit with your pearls. If you can come I'll arrange to introduce you now."

He left at once through the anteroom, walking past a client, who turned the pages of a magazine as a woman three blocks away would be doing.

Outside the bank the gingko tree had spread its leaves like tiny hands.

She sat as before inside the gate, presumably wearing Henrietta's pearls. The gate was unlocked and he stepped inside. She was dressed not in the usual black but today in a feminine pale gray suit, with the jacket removed and draped across the back of her chair. The blouse she wore was a creamy white, narrowly ruffled and very low cut. The breast and the pearls were framed in ruffles. He found he was deeply moved at the sight. She wore the pearls in a special way. He supposed it would be a professional way. For she did not seem to claim them at all or to feel her beauty enhanced by them. Rather, her fair flesh simply displayed them. He could not take his eyes from her skin, which beneath his gaze seemed to kindle and flush. She was caught in the act of turning a page, her eyes downcast as they ever had been.

Miss Doyle stood by like a proper duenna. "Miss Iris Medlock. Mr. Richard Barclay." She turned to him. "I have told her about your aunt and her wishes."

"Since she cannot meet you herself . . ." he began. He stopped, for she had raised her eyes. They were deepest violet, a shade he had never encountered before. And he saw in them that she was older than he had guessed. There was something not bold but touched with a knowledge that matched his own. They held him a moment and then released him. Before they did so, something he shared with them seemed to swoon. No words could describe it. He could not speak.

Miss Doyle was holding the gate for him.

He left in a state of intoxication. In his life in the world he had dealt with facts. Or so he had thought. He saw it now: he had dealt with shadows. He walked away from the sole reality. The only space was the space she filled. The only time was the hour between eleven and twelve.

For a while he was content to remain simply caught in her undertow. Just once he allowed himself to go at one of her hours and drink her in as he followed Miss Doyle. She did not raise her eyes to him, but between them something had formed itself. And now, in arranging his coins at night, he began to plan how they would meet. He would be waiting outside the bank. He would join her as she walked away. He could not imagine her elsewhere committed, so contained she seemed as she sat in her chair. And in the one deep look they had shared there were silent professions. He could swear to it.

And then on a Monday his aunt called up. "Richard, I'll need the pearls for the ball. It's a week from today."

His heart sprang up. It was Iris Medlock's week with them. "Of course," he said. "I'll get them out and bring them around." He blessed his aunt for providing his chance.

He arranged to get them out on Wednesday, of course between eleven and twelve. The day was warm. Stalls had opened with fruit to sell. The clothes that people wore in the street were as bright as the tulips that lined the walks and the quince that bloomed beyond the gates. It gave him pleasure to wonder what she was wearing today. Possibly he would stand before her, watching her gently incline her head, watching her raise her arms like wings to work the clasp at the back of her neck, watching the pearls tumble into her hand. Possibly she would hold them out. In taking them he would know her touch.

Beside the door the gingko tree was full of itself.

He was puzzled to find she was not in her place. He approached Miss Doyle. "My aunt has ordered her pearls," he smiled.

As she opened the box he remarked to her with elaborate ease, "I assumed Miss Medlock would have them on."

She glanced at him briefly and petted her hair. "Miss Medlock is no longer with us," she said.

He was stunned at her words. "But why?" he asked.

She shrugged and pinched the waves in her hair. "I believe she said she was leaving town . . . Of course the bank will take care of it. We have a short list of women who sit. The delay is simply in bonding one and arranging schedules, all of that. You will not be billed for today, of course."

He was in a turmoil of balked desire akin to grief. He slipped the pearls in their velvet case into his pocket and left the bank. By the lobby clock he saw it was only half past eleven, but he wandered into a small cafe where he usually ate his simple lunch. He sat in the corner and ordered coffee, black, to drink. He brushed away the proffered menu. He found he was too disturbed to eat.

Sipping his coffee, he began to think there was something strange in the sudden departure of Iris Medlock. Why would she undertake to sit with Henrietta's pearls unless she had not known at the time how brief an engagement it would be? Or perhaps—a sobering thought occurred—those pearls had inspired her disappearance. He tried to crush an ugly doubt as unworthy of her and of himself, of the thing he had vowed to himself they shared. But he could not finally shake it off. He opened the box and looked at the pearls. They seemed to him somehow faintly . . . changed. Although he must confess to himself that he had not looked at them closely before.

He possessed a logical, orderly mind, but suddenly he could not think. There flashed before him the scene at the cove, the diver kneeling before his aunt, and with it the later, joyous return when his uncle, who had taken a dive of sorts, had knelt with his fifty-fold precious gift.

He all but staggered when he arose. He walked straight out to a jeweler he knew, one whose profits he had increased, perhaps not fifty-fold, but a lot. As his profits increased his health declined. He was always referring to his estate as if his death had taken place.

"Kline," Richard said, holding out to him the velvet case, "I need to know about these pearls, what they are worth, that sort of thing. They belong to my aunt, who wants them insured."

"Can it wait?" Kline asked in the frailest of tones.

"I'm sorry. I find I'm in rather a bind."

Kline took the pearls with a trembling hand and inserted the little black tube in his eye, whereupon he withdrew to a world composed of a single pearl, the universe in a grain of sand. Beneath his gaze he moved the strand, touching and turning each world in turn, as if he were telling his beads in prayer. His hand had become as steady as rock.

Before he emerged the answer was clear. But Richard must hear it in all its horror. "Tell me," he said.

The eye that had been alone with the pearls now studied Richard with a slightly myopic, reluctant stare. "They are fine," he said. "I have rarely seen such really fine work. The tiny flaws. Irregular sheen. Imperfectly formed, as the pearl is formed."

"They are fake," said Richard.

"I'm afraid they are. But cleverly done. With a certain value because of the craft."

Once outside, Richard walked the streets with a sharp distaste for the leafing trees. The tulips that had rejoiced him of late now seemed to him products of artifice. The spring itself was Judas-false. The girl who had serenely sat with his very life upon her breast was as cheap and false as the pearls he carried inside his pocket. How easily the switch was made, while Doyle was patting and pinching her hair or twisting her key in another's lock!

He could go to the bank with the fraud, of course. Miss Medlock was bonded, so they said. But this would involve the police at once. And through the police his aunt would come to know of her loss and thus of his own duplicity. Deeply he mourned for his aunt and himself and for the shattering of his dream.

People were walking about in the park. A girl was chasing a laughing child. And on the grass not far away a couple was sitting back to back. Their faces smiled. Their eyes were closed . . . To his anger he found there were tears in his eyes.

Perhaps if he moved with all possible speed he could recover the stolen gems. Perhaps he might even recover his dream. Perhaps by some unaccountable chance it was not she who had switched the pearls. He found himself wishing with all his heart that Doyle had done the nefarious deed. Perhaps she had tricked the innocent Iris. At any rate, he knew that he must confront Miss Medlock.

But first he had to confront Miss Doyle. He summoned his best have-a-look-at-your-stock-portfolio manner, designed to inspire implicit trust. Before she could reach for her sovereign key he interposed with the gracious request. "My aunt has a little favor to ask. She was more than charmed with Miss Medlock's service. She declares her pearls are more beautiful than ever and would like to send her a little token. My aunt would simply like her number so that she may call and ask where she may send the gift. That is, if Miss Medlock is still in the city."

Miss Doyle had a look of glass in her eye. "The bank has never found it to be in anyone's interest . . ."

"I may add," he went on, "that I have seen the gift. It is lovely. A tiny brooch surrounded by pearls. She has had it for years, but now she insists Miss Medlock must have it."

"I might look for the number and call your aunt."

"My aunt," he said, "is not taking calls. She is somewhat ill. It is why she has asked me to do this for her . . . and why I feel I must humor her."

It gave him the fiercest pleasure to lie. Miss Doyle was punching the waves in her hair.

He said, "I think we must act at once or Miss Medlock will have left the city." It occurred to him as a possible thing that the two of them had arranged it together. Perhaps Miss Medlock was a plant of Doyle's.

She pressed her iron-gray locks for an answer, cajoling them with an urgent hand. At last she wilted and gave him the number. He took it away without a word and drove himself to the public library. In the city directory he found the address.

The street was in the older section. Roots of trees had mangled the pavement. Utility lines brutalized the trees. Houses that once had a touch of class were fractured into apartments for rent. In one of these he found her number—up the stairs and on the left.

A pale man, thirtyish, answered the door. Richard could only describe him as seedy. A shapeless sweater with pockets that sagged. Horn-rimmed glasses with an earpiece gone.

"Miss Medlock," said Richard. "Miss Iris Medlock."

The glasses tilted and a hand flew up to adjust the angle. Behind the man a bird cage tilted at a similar angle. He stared at Richard without expression. Slowly and faintly he shook his head.

Richard was almost prepared to leave. He stepped back to scan the door for the number, when the man gave a quick, nervous glance behind. "She's here now, isn't she?" Richard said. Before he pushed his way into the room he was struck with the anguish of why he was there. The room was empty except for the bird, who fluttered and chirped in its tilted cage.

"She doesn't live here," said the fellow behind him.

Without the slightest hesitation Richard crossed the room to open a door. She was sitting on the side of an unmade bed, wearing jeans and a turtleneck jersey that covered the charms of throat and chest. Her eyes were haunted with something that seemed to him resignation. He could not speak. There was only a long, sad look between them. It told him that she had been aware how long he had lingered before the gate . . . and how she had dwelt in his days and his dreams.

Then she shuddered slightly. Her full lip quivered. A wave of hair fell across her cheek.

The man at once interposed himself. "I must ask you to leave, whoever you are." Richard had the impression that the man had guessed who he was from the start.

"Who is this man?" Richard asked her now. When she did not reply, he felt relief. It left him free to scan her companion's sallow face for a family resemblance and find it there. Indeed, he almost petitioned it there.

The man was shrilling his indignation. "I shall call the police unless you leave."

"I wouldn't advise that," Richard said and watched the two of them swiftly crumble. She put her hands to her face and wept.

He drew the case from his inside pocket. "These pearls are not my aunt's. They are fake. I have had them appraised. They are nothing at all."

He could hear the bird in the room behind him hurl itself against the cage. He found it hard to endure her tears. He said at last, "Give me the pearls that belong to my aunt and I'll go away. Nothing will happen. I'll simply go."

If anything, she was stricken the more.

And now her companion advanced upon him. "All right," he said.
"All right, all right." He adjusted his glasses and steadied a lens between thumb and finger. "She took the pearls but she put them back. I had them appraised. They were nothing but paste and she put them back." His voice began to unravel a bit. "Why would we steal anything that was paste? What did you have in mind?" he said. "Collecting insurance and blaming her, when all the time they were nothing but paste? That is a neat little trick I'll say!"

She had thrown herself back on the unmade bed. A pale blue coverlet framed her face. Her eyes were closed but streaming tears. Defenseless beauty overthrown. The mermaid being reclaimed by the sea.

Richard looked away to harden his heart. "Of course," he said, "this is what you would say . . . Nevertheless, I want my pearls."

"You have them, man!"

Richard turned to him. "Then give me the others, the ones that you used to make the switch."

"All right, all right! But I tell you they are nothing but paste."

"We shall see," said Richard. "We shall indeed."

"Iris, where did you put the things?"

She sat up straight. "You took them," she said in a desolate voice that was thick with tears. Never before had he heard her voice. It seemed to come from beneath the sea. It thrust her far beyond his reach.

There followed what seemed a frantic search. Of course, Richard thought, they must make it good . . . They have probably left them with a fence. They probably have the money in hand. At last he sank to the unmade bed to watch with detachment the frenzied hunt. An opening, shutting, and tossing about, a frothing of male and female attire. He was forced to observe, from the speed with which the blend was accomplished, how exceptionally close their arrangements were. He noted how shapely her body was, how graceful all her movements could be. His mother would sing a song that ran: ". . . so fair and yet so false was she." The ridiculous words were in his head. Over and over they sang themselves.

The room appeared to exfoliate, then fall in a heap like a rose that is spent, until it resembled the unmade bed.

And suddenly they produced the pearls. The sight of them caught him so by surprise that he was fairly slow to rejoice. Sitting there, he had kissed them away. She wiped her eyes and blew her nose. Her companion stood with his glasses atilt. The bird in the cage began to chirp. They acted, he thought, as if all were well.

He had to confess a certain confusion. He asked himself why he did not phone the police at once. But then he recalled he had promised her he would go away. He longed for a peaceful end to it all. But something said it was far from over. Something said it might never end. To straighten his mind he said to her slowly, "You left the bank because of the switch. You thought my aunt would discover it."

Her companion broke in, "She left because I discovered your pearls were paste, and I saw she was being set up for the rap."

"Well, well," said Richard. He smiled at them. "You wish to plant your fraud on me. But you waste your breath. My aunt has worn these pearls for years." He opened the case he held in his hand and replaced one strand of pearls with another. "Nevertheless, I shall take them both."

Extravagantly she cried to him, "Take the key and lock us in. How can we leave? Then you will see."

"What shall I see?" he asked her gently, seeing her in the bank once more, in the innocence of her rose-sweet flesh locked from him behind the gate.

"You'll see that we are right," she said. The tears that stood in her eyes were pearls.

He shook his head and left the room. And he knew that what they had searched for and found or seemed to have searched for and seemed to have found might well be one of a dozen strands that served to further their joint career. He knew this and yet he walked away. To save but an ember of his dream to blow alive sometimes at night. And because there was something else in his head. The end of the song his mother would sing: ". . . so fine and yet so false was he." The line had echoes he must explore.

His final image was that of a bird clinging for life to his tilted perch.

He drove to a jeweler whose shop he had seen but one whom he had never employed. "I have a string of pearls," he said, producing the one that had just been given. "Can you tell me if they are genuine?"

The jeweler looked at them sharply and smiled and looked at them sharply once again. "They're paste," he said. "You didn't know?"

Richard's heart was bleak. In spite of himself he had not despaired. Now he supposed he would call the police. But what would it serve in the sum of things? He had small hope of restoring to Henrietta her pearls. She would never recover her faith in life or her faith in him. Perhaps it was best to let it ride. Perhaps she would never discover the truth. But who could guess? Who could tell what knowledge a long communion with the pearls had bought? He prayed to God she would never know.

But now he must lay all doubts to rest. He drew the other strand from his vest. "And what about these? They belong to my aunt, who broke them once and had them restrung. She suspects there may have been substitutions. Could you tell if any of these are false?" He swore it would be his final lie.

The jeweler laughed. He was a jolly fellow with a rounded face and shoulders rounded from plying his trade. "I see. With the first you were testing me. But these will take a little longer. I shall have to examine each pearl in turn."

"Of course," said Richard. "It is what I wish."

The jeweler smiled with great good humor. He ducked and emerged with a little book. "Here is something may interest you. Read about pearls while I look at these."

Richard was far too tense to read, but he turned a leaf, seeing the hand of Iris Medlock, the careless way it had with a page. He had an impression of bluest waters, grayish cliffs, and naked bodies against the sky. And in his mind was the double image, like two sides of a single coin: the diver kneeling with the marriage pearl . . . his uncle kneeling with fifty more.

The jeweler was back and shaking his head. There was nothing jolly about his words. "I'm afraid," he said, "your aunt has been swindled. I trust it was no one in this city. All of the pearls are paste but one." He pinched it briefly between his fingers.

Richard recalled his aunt's insistence that she could tell which pearl was the first.

So fine and yet so false was he . . . Perhaps she had known it all these years, and her heart had looked the other way. The scoundrel, he thought. I always knew that for all his airs he was not worth one of her little fingers. And Richard was compelled to add as he entered once more the fulsome spring: Neither am I . . . neither am I.

He would never recall which pearl it was. One genuine thing, one bead of truth in the lives of them all, and already it had escaped him.

Water into Wine

Bees were ravishing the yellow Lady Banksia roses that fringed her doorway. He'd been instructed to greet the ladies with a pleasantry. "Ma'am, you got a lot of bees." He held his coffee-colored briefcase in one hand and the matching case with his equipment in the other.

"I sure have," she said. "They keep me company."

She waited for him then, her eyes squinting through the late morning sunlight, noting his slick-backed graying hair and his sun-tanned, sort of skinny face. She could see his gray Chevy in the yard beyond. It had mud on the fenders.

He backed away from the bees and put down the case, which seemed to be heavy. "Ma'am, I represent the Crystal Clear Water Corporation. The Crystal Clear people have authorized me to give a limited number of families in this area a test of their water for its purity. This is absolutely free. No obligation. Absolutely free." He said it with care, stepping over the words, as if he had to step over them to get past her door.

"I got no reason to worry about my water," she said.

"Ma'am, I'm real happy to hear about that." He had been instructed not to argue with them. Make it through the door. Make it to the faucet . . . "I say that because the others down the road didn't test too good. Maybe it would help us to look around and see what you're doin' right."

She studied him with narrowed eyes. She listened to the bees.

His own eyes were on the words he was about to say. "We have a scientific interest."

"Look around where?"

"Well, ma'am, I'd like to test your water where you get it from the tap. Won't take but a minute. A very interesting test. It might interest you to watch." He smiled at her hopefully, trying to read her face through the grids of the screen.

She knew there was a chance that he wasn't what he said. But the way she felt, she didn't much care. She was hanging somewhere between brave and scared, not going either way, just stuck between, and lonesome as well. So when he smiled at her she let him in.

She led him through the front door and into her kitchen. She was conscious of herself, of looking too skinny in her knitted shirt and jeans, of being all of thirty and looking older. She was conscious that he might have a gun in that case, a rope to tie her up with, and plenty of room inside to carry off what he stole.

When he opened it up on the kitchen counter it contained small bottles and a very large one that had a hose attachment and was full of white beads. He did not look around but went straight for the faucet and turned it on and off. "Ma'am," he said, "would you have a couple of jars, any size?" You had to use theirs or they thought it was a trick. Thought you coated yours with something before you left home.

"I hope you don't aim to mess up my kitchen."

She found some clean jars for him under the sink, let him take his pick. All the time she was thinking that she wouldn't be doing this if Buck hadn't left. If Buck hadn't left she'd be keeping the baby that was his inside her safe. She wouldn't be opening her farmhouse door and letting in a man she had never seen . . . Buck, you ever comin' back? He had looked across the field with his fresh-polished boot on the step of his rig. Well, honey, this haul is gonna take some time . . . And the way he said it . . .

There was a knot in her throat as she laid the jars in a line on the counter. But nothing in this world had ever made her cry.

He lifted two of her jars and held them up to the light. Then he brought her a chair from the kitchen table, as if she were a lady in a dress, all of that. "I want you to sit and be comfortable."

"I understood you said this wouldn't take but a minute." She ignored the chair.

"Sometimes it takes maybe two." He smiled at her in an uncertain way, as if he was afraid that she might not watch. His eyes were sad.

From the gray in his hair she thought he could be about forty or more. He was wearing a green tie and a dark brown suit that had a snag on the sleeve and a shine from wear. Buck was always dressed . . . well, like he was going to a dance in town. Blue suede jacket. Fancy shirt. Polished boots. Even for a haul he dressed like that. You lookin' for to catch a girl? she said.

She circled the chair, she didn't know why, and then sat down. Sort of like a dog in the grass, she thought. She did a lot of things that she didn't know why. She ran her fingers through her short brown hair. It was sticky from the jelly she had made the day before. He seemed relieved and smiled at her again. His eyes inside the sad were very shy.

"Ma'am, your husband around somewhere? I'd really like to show him this demonstration." Always get the husband if you can, they said. He had the pay.

She looked away. "He's out and around. I really couldn't say where."

But don't insist. Makes the woman think you don't value her judgment . . . He nodded and swiftly drew from his case the bottle with the beads and the hose attached. He fastened one end to the mouth of her faucet and turned on the water, which bubbled through the beads and into a jar he had chosen from her store. He placed the jar of water carefully before her, as if he couldn't bear to spill a single drop. His hand was shaking just a little she saw.

The hens were shrieking, more than likely at a hawk circling overhead. Or the black cat had gotten in their nests again . . . She might be shrieking with them before this was done.

"This bottle," he said, touching it reverently, "contains the elements we find in every Crystal Clear Purifier sold today." He recited it rhythmically like a poem.

She sighed and stirred. "I ain't seen nothin' that amazed me yet."

He smiled as if her comment gave him special delight. He lifted the other jar and filled it nearly full with water from the faucet. His hands were awkward. The knuckles were red. "This is your water as you drink it from the faucet . . . This other is your water treated with our product. Now watch," he said. He drew forth one of his bottles from the case. He shook it with a flourish, up and down and sideways, making a thing of it, and all the time smiling into the sink. Then with the dropper attached to the lid he measured three drops into the second of the jars. "This is your water we have treated with our product." He dropped three drops into the other jar. It began to grow troubled before their eyes. "This is your water as you drink it from the tap." From the troubled water there emerged a cloud of milky apparitions that swam like fish, then settled to the bottom.

She looked at them steadily with eyes like glass. "You expectin' me to shriek or somethin' like that?"

"No, ma'am, I'm not. You're a sensible woman. You wouldn't shriek, but you wouldn't drink. You'd understand that what you are seein' is impurities you take into your body each and every day." He looked at her with a kind of dumb pleading, like a dog who wants something dumped in his dish. "The chemical in this bottle has coated and weighted those impurities."

"My husband," she told him, her eyes growing merry, "he wouldn't take kindly to what all you're sayin' about the water in his well."

"Ma'am, no offense. No offense intended. Just a demonstration that's a service we give."

He picked up the jar with the milky apparitions and swirled them into a lively chase, then let them sink once more to the bottom. It seemed to be fun. His mouth went happy. But his eyes were thoughtful and sad and shy. He raised the water to his nose and sniffed. She could tell that he thought of making a face but decided he wouldn't just to be polite.

She began to enjoy it. She hadn't enjoyed a thing since Buck had left. "You want a cup of coffee?" she said to him.

He smiled at her sweetly and warily. His eyes were green with flecks of brown. One of them had a small cast in it. "I'm obliged for your hospitality . . . if you make it from a batch I can purify."

She laughed out loud. "How much you askin' for this thing you sell?"

But he wouldn't say yet. "I'd like to give you a further demonstration if you have the time." He selected another two jars from her stock and filled them with water, just as before. With an air of intrigue he chose a bottle from the ones in the case. With a little spoon, which he drew from his pocket, he measured a spoonful into each jar and stirred it thoughtfully. He stirred it red. He paused for a moment to let her react.

"Like turnin' water into wine," she said.

He nodded his approval. "I see you know your Bible."

"Not exactly," she said.

"It's vegetable dye." He was open about it. "Now, here," he said, "is what I want you to see. Here we have a little chart." He handed it to her. "It measures the pollution by how many drops of this liquid in my bottle will turn the red back into clear."

With elaborate care he put a drop in the water that had bubbled through beads and stirred till it was colorless. With a show of reluctance he began adding drops to the untreated water, counting them out in a hesitant manner, stirring each with a hopeful whirl. Suddenly the wine was back into water.

"Twenty," he announced. His voice was sad. He looked away from her into the room. "Now shall we look at the chart you have?" He had joined her at the chair. His clothes smelled of chemical laced with cheese. With the baby inside, her nose was keen. "Twenty drops . . ." His red-knuckled finger traced it across. "Read for yourself, ma'am: 'Extremely polluted. As in water from a pond.'

"Ma'am, he said, "what can I say?"

"Say I'm droppin' dead this minute," she said. She put both hands to her throat and choked.

"Oh, ma'am," he said, "we got to be serious."

"I am," she said, laughing. "I been feelin' rotten. I thought it was this baby I got inside." Her merriment broke and she looked away. She couldn't believe she had told about the baby, but she did a lot of things she didn't know why.

He shook his head and looked into the sink. "Ma'am, I don't need to tell you how important it is when you carry a child to have water as pure as can be to drink . . . I'm sure your husband can appreciate that."

She got up and walked to the door. She watched the brown hens scratching outside. She said, "I been drinkin' it all my life. When my baby comes . . ." She broke off then. "I don't have the money for what you're sellin', whatever you're askin'. That settles it, don't it?"

But he wouldn't say. He turned on the faucet and let the water bubble away through the beads and out of the hose and into the sink. He caught a splash of it into a jar and held it out to her graciously. "Would you care to have a taste of this water?" he said. "Just to compare . . ."

"I ain't thirsty," she said.

He watched her sadly. He seemed at a loss. She figured he had plumb run out of his act. At last he said, "You know this pollution, it might be sittin' right here in this house. In the pipes inside. The water might actually be good from the well. I've seen it happen. Would you give me permission to test it at the pump? It would make you feel better . . . now, wouldn't it, ma'am?"

"I feel fine," she said. She did not turn around. She was mad at herself for bringing in the baby. He waited a bit. She heard him at the front door. Then she heard him on the gravel, headed for the pump. She listened to the bees. They had hives in back and a field full of clover, but they seemed to want to hang around her door all day. She liked them around. She could dream them into the hum of Buck's rig rounding the curve, coming down the hill.

It wasn't five minutes until he was back. She waited for him to tell her it was just as bad and the only thing left was to buy his machine. She heard him say in a different voice, "I'm makin' us some wine out of what I got . . ." Like the two of them were fixing to have them a real fun time.

She was turning to tell him she'd had enough when she heard glass shatter and felt the spray of wet through her jeans. The jar with the milky stuff was broken at her feet. He was standing by the sink with the jar of red water. He laid it down and clutched at the counter. She saw his legs buckle slowly beneath him. His face and neck had gone grayer than ash. He was on his knees then and trying to breathe.

"Mister?" she said. "Mister? Somethin' wrong?"

He coughed and gazed at her in resignation. He said it thickly: "Got stung at the door."

"You allergic to bee sting, somethin' like that?"

He nodded slowly. His eyes had closed.

She was thinking fast. "Mister, you got any medicine for this?"

"Car . . ." he said and lay on her brown and white linoleum floor.

She turned and ran for his car outside. The trunk was ajar. Nothing inside it but tools and tires and rubber boots. She opened the glove box and dragged out its contents—maps and maps, a greasy rag, four packs of gum. Stuck to the dashboard was the photograph of a little boy . . .

She ran back to the house. He lay on his side, one arm beneath him. She dropped to her knees. "Mister," she said, "I couldn't find no medicine." She went through his coat and the pockets of his pants. "You got to start breathin'. You hear me, sir?" She struck his back. "You got to breathe, mister."

He drew a shallow breath. It was like Buck shifting gears on a hill, then abruptly a silence, then a flutter in the chest and a long-drawn sigh. When she loosened his tie, she felt the hammer beat of his heart. "Mister, it's time you breathed again." But he lay like a rock. She pushed him slowly onto his back. "Mister, don't do this, don't die on me. I had just about all kinda stuff I can take. You walk in here and then die on me?"

The broken glass had cut his lip. She pulled his mouth open and lowered her own to cover his. She drew a deep breath and waited and emptied it into him. She had never done such a thing before. With a little shock she tasted his blood. But again she poured herself into a stranger. Over and over, until he was Buck. His mouth was Buck's. It was not her breath but the baby's breath. And now she could feel the drag of the rig as it turned around to come home to them.

She fell exhausted onto the floor. When she turned her head she could feel the rise and fall of the chest. "Mister, you hear me talkin' to you?" He gave no sign. The wet from the jar was in her hair.

After a while she got up and rang a doctor's number she found in the book. His office was twenty-five miles away. He was out on call, the nurse explained. When he telephoned in, she would let him know. "Well, ma'am, he don't talk. I can't make 'im talk." A kid was yelling close to the phone, and the nurse was crooning, "Ain't you 'shamed, makin' all that fuss! Lie down and let me put your didies back on." She raised her voice. "Sounds like he's in a coma to me. You better watch out to see that he don't quit breathin' again."

She swept up the glass and mopped the floor. The sun was well into afternoon. She made a liverwurst sandwich and sat in the kitchen chair close beside him, eating it slowly and watching him breathe, watching the sun through the kitchen window brush the rundown heels of his shoes, then creep to cover the rest of him. His coat and pants had died on him. They settled against his body and legs like a parachute that has hit the ground. A quiver moved in his throat and chest. There were lines about his eyes and mouth. And in the hollows below his cheeks she stared at shadows deep in the bone. She was hearing the engine hum of the rig moving farther and farther away . . . Buck, we better get married now. Oh? How come? he wanted to know. Well, Buck, we started a baby now . . . He was playing cards, with the dark outside and wind and all. He said he used to be a gambling man. You know I can't take that, he said. He shuffled a while and laid them out on the kitchen table. Married or gettin' a baby, Buck? He played him a hand like maybe the cards would say which one. And when he was through he scooped them up and walked outside and let them all go one by one, blowing away in the windy night. Buck, how come? You blowin' me and the baby away? Some a them cards I found next day was drowned in the pond below the house.

Suddenly she heard the sound of a motor. Her heart leapt up. But at once she knew that it wasn't the rig. She went to the door. A heavy-set man was pulling himself from a blue station wagon. He walked, slow and slinky, over to the Chevy and looked inside and then he looked inside the trunk. He kicked a rear tire and spat in the weeds. "This the Ames's house?" he called to her.

She waited a little. "How come you wanta know?"

"Well, I'm Sam Grimes from Crystal Clear Water. I'm tryin' to track my salesman down. I see you got his car in yore front yard. You got him stashed somewhere inside?" He was pale curly headed and broad in the beam. His sleeves were rolled up. His tie was looped into a purple noose. The sun had barbecued his face.

Without a word she let him in. He smelled of snuff. He whistled when he saw the figure stretched out on the kitchen floor. "You give 'im too much bad water to drink? Never seen it lay a man out before."

"I'm mighty glad you got here, mister. I talked to a nurse. He got some kinda family should be notified?"

He gave the kitchen a quick once-over and held the red water up to the light, as if it were some of the jelly she'd made. "I wouldn't hardly know about that." He studied the man on the floor with interest. "What ails 'im?" he said.

"He said a bee stung 'im. Then he hit the floor."

"Seem like he lost a little blood." He stared at her with a curious smile. "Maybe you slugged 'im for gittin' fresh."

"It's like I said."

Grimes shook his head. "Man, I tell you, this boy I tried to he'p 'im but his luck's run out. I come for his equipment. Been trackin' 'im all day. Ain't made a sale all week. That's Monday through Friday he ain't made a sale." He paused and looked at her warily. "He sold you a machine?"

"I got no money."

"There you are. He don't use his judgment, which I don't think he's got. I can give one look, see a party ain't good for a sale and move on. Not him, he kills half a day."

He jerked his pants up and settled them a bit. He leaned against the counter, embracing his arms that were rusty with sun. "He's the kind of individual can't sell a damn thing. I got a brother-in-law like that. Somebody was to say you can't git into heaven without you got this particular item cost you ten cents, he couldn't make a sale."

"Mister, you gotta put 'im in your car and get 'im to a doctor 'fore he dies on us. He quit breathin' on me once."

Grimes shook his head. He touched his grilled cheek with a tender hand. "Got a real tight schedule. Gotta take his equipment to a boy out in Leeds used to sell for me and git back for a meetin'. You try that nurse again."

"You mean you gonna walk out that door and leave a man on my floor I don't even know his name?"

"Name's Greeley. Joe Greeley. Got some Greeleys live around here but I don't think he's kin. Come from somewheres else . . . When he come to, you tell 'im I been here and took his case. His briefcase, too. 'Cep' it ain't his. Belongs to me, you understand."

She stifled her panic and set her jaw. "You walk out on me I'm gonna damn your eyes." It surprised her the way it flew out of her, as if it were waiting there to be said. Inside of her maybe she meant Buck, too.

He threw back his head and hooted at her. "Cuss away, little lady! I'm gonna try to bear up. Now, the best I can do, we put 'im in his car and you head somewhere."

"And have 'im quit breathin' on me on the road!"

"You want 'im to quit breathin' on me, that it?"

She turned away in despair. He was stashing bottles inside the case. He zipped open the briefcase and riffled the contents. "Here's a letter that looks to be his." He tossed it onto the counter for her.

She turned and faced him. "You gotta help me get 'im onto the bed."

He winked at her slowly, "You want 'im in yore bed, we'll put 'im there for sure. He's liable to be a disappointment, though."

As he drove away she stood looking down at the man he had dumped on her blue bedspread. The move to the bed had unsettled his breathing. It was coming at intervals in soft dry sobs. She took off his loafers run down at the heels and then his coat. She remembered the letter Grimes had left on the counter. She fetched it from the kitchen and opened it and read. It was a one-page note in a woman's hand: "You want to see your kid you send me his support. You said you got a job, you make a sale and send it. Till you do stay away."

She read it three times. Then it struck her in the stomach where her baby lay. God, Buck, you wanta see 'im, you got a key to the door. I wouldn't charge you money to see your own kid. Like a sideshow or somethin' you pay to get in . . .

She folded the letter and stuffed it in the coat at the foot of the bed. It was late afternoon. The hens were clucking in a chorus under the window. They hadn't been fed. She heard the long wail of the lone Jersey cow coming in from the field and ready to be milked. No way I can 'tend to the whole damn world. She said aloud to the baby inside, "When you come out, you try real hard to get your breath, and keep on breathin' and don't need mine. I'm liable not to have any left."

She found thread and a needle and sat by the bed to sew up the snag on the sleeve of the coat. The hum of Buck's rig was in her mind, as it always was whenever she sat. The thrust of the engine, the giant wheels, eighteen in all, rolling right over her to crush her breath . . . Buck, if someone was to get in your way, you reckon you could stop it in time? she said. That depends, little girl, on how close they was . . .

What about me? I'm close . . . I'm close . . .

She stared at the bed. Already she had forgotten his name. His face had turned gray and his breathing had stopped. She dropped his coat. She fell like a stone upon his mouth. His lips were dry and familiar to her. And nothing about them was Buck's at all. The mouth was his own. The life was his own. It flowed with the life of the baby in her. She gave up her breath through no will of her own. She was faint with the giving. She felt in their bodies the struggle to live, but deep in the man, more familiar now than his mouth to her, something that said he didn't want to live. It joined with the dark inside herself, with the hum of the rig moving farther away, with the cards gone down in the mud of the pond like the things that had swirled and sunk in the jar, and she clung to him wanting them both to die . . . But the baby inside her cried out to be born . . . to be given his breath.

She fell away from him onto the bed. Her head was reeling, caught up into a whirl of dust till she didn't know who she was or why. After a moment she reached for him. She threw one arm across his chest. She felt it faintly rise and fall. It was like she was on the bed with her daddy, telling him to try real hard to live. But he wouldn't try. He wanted to die. It had just come spring and the whole outdoors was full of sun. The jessamine flowers smelled so sweet they were in her throat and on her tongue. They tasted of how it was sweet to die . . .

And now she lay as still as if she had died herself. She didn't know why she fought so hard to make them live, when all the time they wanted to die or something inside them wanted to die or ride away from her down the road and that was as good as dead to her. I guess I'm scared a bein' left alone. Me and the bees and the cow and the hens, and my little baby comin' outta me, sayin', Mama, how come nobody around?

She must have slept, for she grew aware that the light had failed. The room was shadowed. The sparrows were nesting under the eaves, and a small gray owl that came at dusk was in his place and gave his call from the topmost branch of the sycamore tree. It seemed to her that Buck was there. He was back and lay beside her now. She couldn't remember when he had come or how it had been with him till now. She only knew that waking to him was the realest and best she could hope to have. A long singing began in her. It was in her throat and arms and breast. "Buck?" she said, and the singing died. "Buck?" she whispered. And then she woke to the way it was.

The man beside her did not stir except to breathe. She listened to him with all the singing gone out of her, the sound of it faint in the hum of the rig and moving farther and farther away. Her sadness rose and then lay down with the baby and slept. The gray owl called. "Mister?" she said. "You hear me now?"

She waited till the room was dark and cool. She spoke again. "You hear me now?" And when she was sure that he wouldn't hear a single thing she said, she began to talk. She circled herself. She talked about the cow who ached to be milked and the hens on the nests with nothing to eat. They just have to make it till morning, she said. Things come up that you don't expect. She circled around till she came to Buck, and then the words were a great relief. Like walking through water in summertime.

Two years ago she had found him in a diner down the road a ways. He was in the middle of a cross-country haul. Golden hair and sweet to see. Sweet to hear him with a country talk that was different from hers. Texas, he said. A bit of Nevada. Called his eighteen-wheeler Baby Doll. Loved her like a woman. When he found the right woman he could love her more. Her car was stalled. That's why she was in there looking for help. I can give you a lift if it's on my way. She let him take her clear to her house. She wanted him to see how nice it was, and all of it hers since her daddy died . . . You ever comin' back? she said to him. She kept the lonely out of her voice. Sure, he said. Comin' through next month. You give me a call, you hear, she said. I'll fix you dinner. Better than the diner I guarantee. He leaned his head out of the cab at that and grinned at her where she stood in the road. You must not eat your cookin', little girl . . . Skinny or not, I can cook, she said.

Never knew when he would come or go. It was good when he came . . . Buck, you ever comin' back? Like I said the first time. I was standin' out there in the road again. Just like at first. Same place in the road . . . Well, honey, this haul is gonna take some time . . . Left me five hundred in the dresser drawer.

I never cried in my life, not once. You could ask my daddy before he died. No way you gonna catch me cryin' now . . .

A wind was moving in the cottonwood tree that stood on the bank beside the house. Its leaves in a whisper rose to a chatter. A branch of the sugarberry brushed the screen . . . Buck, it's funny the way you and me turned out. You makin' this haul that's gonna take forever. Me lyin' beside a half-dead man that any minute could breathe his last. I heard it said somethin' bad like this gives a baby inside you a mark somewhere . . .

The branch had brushed the screen again. It seemed to her that the man beside her knew the sound. It seemed to slice across them both. It was not that he moved or his breathing changed. It was like a door being opened at last. She lay quite still, and shy of a presence that received her own. It was nothing like Buck being Buck, more Buck, taking what she was and chewing it up till he swallowed her. Awake or asleep he swallowed her.

Slowly her caution began to fade. She lay beside him, knowing he was like the baby inside her, taking what she gave, leaving her the same. She had changed for Buck but it wasn't enough. Too skinny for him to change to wine. And now his tree was growing in her. The tree at the window, moving shadow, crossed her breast and crossed the breast beside her own. She asked herself if the baby could take the two of them and change the way they were to wine. If wine was better. She guessed it was.

Her eyes were shut, remembering this man, his green eyes flecked with a little brown, and the picture of the boy inside the car, and his awkward hands making water into wine just so he could turn it to water again. The kind of trick you would do for a kid . . . She wished there was some kind of magic like that to do with what you had to say, to make it better than you knew to say . . .

She began to speak aloud to the dark: "You ever try to love somebody gone off? Off where you maybe can't see 'im again? When you was havin' a peaceable life and now you got a hole that's bored clean through . . . If you never did, you might could wonder how come me sayin' what I got to say. But I reckon you know. I reckon you do . . . I seen your boy, his little picture inside your car."

She waited a while to get it right. "This house is good. My daddy built it and gave it to me. I got four acres. It's good rich land would raise a crop if someone be around to help with it. Got hens and a cow ain't been fed today. The bees . . . I'd as soon be rid a them bees. When my baby comes, he might get stung.

"I feel like when my baby comes a heap a things gonna worry me lots. And a lots more things used to worry me won't do it now. Like am I skinny, things like that. I'll just be lookin' to keep my baby from bein' skinny. Things like that. I reckon you know it better than me."

She laid her hand on the baby asleep. And now it was easy to tell of him. "It's a good baby I got inside me. They don't come any better, any prettier. Got yellow hair and soft brown eyes, and nothin' about him you'd want to change. Lovin' hearted. Lovin' hearted. The one best thing you could say for him . . ." She thought a bit. "Anybody is his he will cleave to that person. He's never gonna let that person go. Come hell or high water, he won't let go. Or never leave . . . won't never leave. Somebody was to take him, he'd find his way home."

She could see the car lights from the road flowing like milk down the wall beside her. She heard the owl winging into a branch above the roof.

"It scares me some, me havin' this baby. Somethin' I never done before. Scared I might not get it right . . ." She was thinking of the boy in the picture in the car and trying to guess how old he was and what he was like when he was born. She could almost see him when he was born. She couldn't see her own baby half so clear.

She didn't know why but she said aloud, "I wish my baby would favor your boy." And when she'd said it she knew it was true. But why it was true she didn't know. Outside, the tree frogs talked of rain. "I know you ain't gonna forget your boy. I know you couldn't if you was to try." Her father had told her a long time ago, you save a man's life you can't turn him loose, you got to see to him. You got no choice, you got to see to him. There was nothin' that said that when you did you couldn't be seein' to your own life, too.

She began to time her breath to his. "I know I'm skinny. Buck always said it. Said there wasn't enough of me to love. But this baby inside me is soft and round . . . I'm offerin' you this baby to be his father as long as it seems like you want to be. I'd be around to take care of him, but you wouldn't ever have to look at me . . ."

The owl was muttering into the dark.

"I got a pond down below the house. You could fish with him in the summertime . . . and teach him to skim a rock on the water like a man can do . . . and how to swim. You could love 'im as hard as you wanted to 'cause you wouldn't ever have to let 'im go."

The cottonwood was wild with wind. The cards were blowing away from Buck, far away and into the dark, but she felt the moon alive in the room. Shadows of branches swept her face and swept her down and into sleep. She clung to waking enough to ask: "The things I said, you think I got no cause to say? Some skinny woman with polluted water you never seen before, don't even know . . . Mister, you know me, take it from me. You musta come closer than anybody I ever met. Maybe you could say I needed you . . . needed somebody that needed what I had got to give and maybe my breath was all was left.

"Exceptin' my baby. I got him left. He's like my breath. I got him left to give if I got a mind to do."

She lay still, thinking of all her words. Too many words and they didn't work. Some she didn't know why she said. And then a feeling came over her, stole over her with the sound of rain, that maybe her baby was grown up now and by the bed looking down at them. There wasn't a place he'd sooner be. There wasn't a thing he'd want to change. Into her sleep the man beside her seemed to say, It's good we come in outta the rain . . .

The rain went off somewhere in the night and left the leaves for her to see in the morning light pressed like hands against the screen. She rose and fixed some breakfast for him—bacon and coffee and grits and egg. He came in just as she finished her plate. He had found his coat and straightened his tie. His face had a stubble the color of sand. He gave her a sad and lingering look. The cast in his eye was plain to see.

"Ma'am, I gave you a heap of trouble."

She searched his face. "You could blame it on them bees a mine."

He ate in silence.

She sat before him. She hadn't had time to comb her hair. She smoothed it down, looking into the shiny side of the toaster. She saw the tremor that stirred his hand. "Some boss man come and took your things."

He looked surprised, then closed his eyes and nodded his head.

"I'd a bought it from you if I wasn't afraid of the money," she said.

He nodded again. He drank his coffee and then he stood. The jar of red water was by the sink. He gave it a swift and joyless glance. "I'm obliged for what all you did for me. I reckon it had to be a lot."

He turned at the door. "We're losers," he said. "Put losers together, you don't get a winner." And then she knew he had heard it all.

She stood in the kitchen and listened to him, his feet on the gravel outrunning the bees, the hum of his Chevy fading away. She poured his red water down the sink. I'm not cryin', mister. You see me cryin'?

But after a week he was back again. This time he was at her kitchen door. He eyed the bees in a patch of clover.

When she came to the door he was at a loss. "I see you still got your bees," he said.

"They live here," she said, "the same as me."

Her eyes slid over the snag in his sleeve, which needed another stitch or two. "You want a glass of pollution?" she asked, for a thing to say.

He watched the bees in the patch of clover. "You don't look skinny to me," he said.

"I'll be fillin' out pretty soon," she said. And then she cried and she couldn't stop. One more thing she didn't know why.

ILLINOIS SHORT FICTION